# WHAT THE RAINS FORETOLD

### N. Mohanan

*translated from
the Malayalam original*
Innalathe Mazha
*by*
### Manoj Neelakanthan

NIYOGI
BOOKS

Originally published in Malayalam as *Innalathe Mazha*, 1996
First English translation, 2022

Published by
**NIYOGI BOOKS**
Block D, Building No. 77,
Okhla Industrial Area, Phase-I,
New Delhi-110 020, INDIA
Tel: 91-11-26816301, 26818960
Email: niyogibooks@gmail.com
Website: www.niyogibooksindia.com

Text © M. Sarita Varma
Translation © Manoj Neelakanthan

Editor: K.E. Priyamvada
Design: Nadeem Ahmed
Cover Aaryama Somayaji

ISBN: 978-93-91125-84-4
Publication: 2022

This is a work of fiction. The names, characters and incidents portrayed in it are the work of the author's imagination. Any resemblance to actual persons, living or dead, events or localities, is entirely coincidental.

All rights are reserved. No part of this publication may be reproduced or transmitted in any form or by any means, electronic or mechanical, including photocopying, recording or by any information storage and retrieval system without prior written permission and consent of the Publisher.

Printed at: Niyogi Offset Pvt. Ltd., New Delhi, India

*To my mother and father,
who have been my guides
and inspiration in writing this book.*

# Contents

| | |
|---|---|
| A Declaration | 9 |
| The Scholar's Devious Plot | 26 |
| The Long Walk of the Agnostic | 38 |
| A Providential Sighting | 54 |
| What the Birds Foretold | 69 |
| The Abandoned and the Orphaned | 83 |
| A Folly Repeated | 102 |
| A Brother's Love | 111 |
| The Newborn's Silence | 132 |
| A Challenge and Hope | 141 |
| Lunacy is a Calling | 154 |
| The Legend of the Hills | 159 |
| Epilogue | 169 |

*He has burst into tears,*
*our mountain Almighty.*
*How the blue yonder opens up,*
*spring-scents in its downpour.*
*The rivulets, the furrows*
*are gurgling, so's my little hovel.*

# A Declaration

The shadow of the night had begun to spread into the heart of the jungle. The sky had not yet darkened fully. Yet, the stars twinkled faintly. He walked softly, listening to the murmur of waves lashing gently somewhere in the distance. A river wound its way into the stillness of the night. Thorns and brambles lay overgrown by the wayside; possibly a road less travelled by, he thought. He was in search of a place to rest for the night. The sound of the waves grew to a gentle splashing as he neared the stream; his instinct had led him to the right place, after all. Overhead, birds chirped from the highest branches of a tree. In the distance a faint primal beat could be heard; melancholic strains of a native ballad, stirrings of a habitation nearby. He found a dilapidated shrine made of stone on the banks of the stream. In the yard facing the shrine was a banyan tree, on a pedestal of raised earth. He sat on the pedestal, exhausted. Suddenly, as if remembering something, he placed his staff and belongings by the tree and walked up to the river. He washed his face, hands and feet and quenched his thirst. By the time he returned to his resting place he was completely exhausted, and flung himself at the foot of the tree. But sleep was nowhere near. He lay there, gazing at the darkening sky. The weariness of his body did not affect his mind. A lesser man would not have embarked upon such a long and arduous journey at such a young age—that too, leaving behind his royal position, privileges and riches. The king had tried his best to dissuade him. It had been a long journey, and yet, it was only the beginning…

\*\*\*

'Hear, hear!' proclaimed the royal messenger to the accompaniment of drums, 'The annual fete for wise men in the state! Winner to be made the Royal Pundit, appointed by His Majesty the King. He shall be offered the exalted seat of wisdom. Gifts, riches and all forms of honour shall be bestowed upon him.'

Far from the scene of proclamation, away from the curious onlookers, and yet near enough to be affected by the event, was a hermitage. A man—no, a boy—stood with head bowed humbly, as though waiting for someone's approval. A closer look revealed youthful features on a grimly set countenance, the shadow of a moustache on his upper lip; the beginnings of youth.

'My son, it takes rigour of an exceptional kind for the quest you want to undertake. Remember, great men have faltered at the task.' But Vararuchi was insistent; he had never been one to feel overwhelmed by challenges. After thirteen years of ascetic life and steadfast devotion at the hermitage, Vararuchi stood at the threshold of enlightenment. The secrets of nature, the gates of knowledge, lay before him, waiting to reveal their secrets.

Now he spoke with quiet determination: 'I wish to pursue and seek Truth.' His words echoed his sincerity. 'Allow me, Sir, to set forth in my quest', he begged.

'The life of a Karmayogi,' continued his master, 'is not an easy one; it demands great strength of character. To understand Mother Nature, and to overcome the frailty of the human condition calls for immense courage and perseverance, my son. May your free spirit and keen insight overcome all hardships....' The Master's hands rested tenderly on the young man's head in blessing. Vararuchi bowed low. He felt strangely light-headed, unaware of the trials and tribulations that awaited him. His journey could now begin.

'Hark, what is that I hear!'

In the distance they heard the rumblings of the proclamation. Master and disciple listened intently.

'The King's invitation to the annual event! Let's go together. It is very propitious that this should mark the beginning of your journey!'

That was how Vararuchi, all of eighteen winters, found himself in the company of wise men who had come from far and near. Hardly anyone in the august gathering would have guessed that this unassuming boy, only a teenager, would end up attracting so much attention by his wit and prowess. Soon the suggestion that he would merely attract attention seemed almost laughable, as the young Vararuchi charmed the audience with his sheer brilliance. He had a solution for every challenge, a reasoning that tore at the heart of every argument. The audience watched spellbound, slowly awakening to the realization that they had a prodigy in their midst.

At the end of the contest, the royal Pundit rose with a daunting question: 'Young man, all of us here are astounded by your brilliance. Now, answer this: which is the most momentous passage in the epic *Ramayana*?

Unflinchingly came the reply:

*'Behold in Rama, Dasharatha your father*
*In Sita, none but me your mother*
*As Ayodhya, in the jungle while*
*And thus at home though in exile*
*Go forth son, peace be with you.'*

'And the most significant line therein?', enquired the King.

Pat came the reply:

*'In Sita, none but me your mother.'*

The entire court arose in great adulation. Above the din of applause, the King announced, 'Congratulations, young man!' Turning to the audience he declared, 'For the first time in the history of our kingdom we have a young man who has been able to defeat all the wise men of our land.' At the heart of the gathering stood the coveted throne, the exalted seat of wisdom, gleaming in white and gold. The King gently urged Vararuchi, 'Would you accept the privilege…' The crowd looked at Vararuchi, hushed with expectation.

But the man of the moment was beset by turmoil. Ecstasy, bewilderment, and reproach enveloped his heart in waves of tumult. He struggled to gain his composure. At long last, grasping for a conviction amid his confusion, he spoke quietly, 'Your Highness, I am indebted to your grace for saying so. But I'm afraid my heart leads me further. In this esteemed company I am but a beginner. On the long road to knowledge I'm a seeker yet.'

Slowly gaining his composure, the young man explained as the crowd listened in disbelief: 'My Lord, I wish to travel around the world, to traverse the ocean of knowledge and discover its distant shore, to understand the labyrinth that is the human condition.' His words grew in eloquence as he strove to describe his longings, 'To loosen the knot of this riddle called life; to arrive at the wellspring of Nature. I was about to set out on my journey, my Lord. It is on my master's insistence that I am here. This was possibly the best start that I could have had in my journey, partaking of the honour of being in such wise company. Allow me, my Lord, to proceed,' Vararuchi implored.

As the audience listened to the young man in stunned silence, Vararuchi bowed low at the feet of his master. He then turned and addressed the gathering: 'Kindly grant me leave and bless my quest.'

Taken aback, the King asked incredulously, 'Is this throne to remain vacant?'

Vararuchi bowed his head.

'If it pleases you, my Lord, I feel completely unworthy of this great honour. I shall return when I find the Truth.'

The King was somewhat appeased by this response. The young man had sought time to become worthy of the royal privilege. So he consented beamingly, 'Excellent, young man! Come back victorious. This seat will remain empty until your return. Meanwhile, if you need my help for anything, the entire kingdom is at your service.'

And thus, Vararuchi strode out of the king's palace.

But in truth, the decision to walk out had not been flippant. The peace he had made, the contentment he had arrived at, had come after a great deal of ordeals and conflicts. Unrest and unease had been his companions as he struggled days and nights to find the meaning to life. The pleasures of this life had beckoned him. He too, had dreamt of an extravagant and prosperous life filled with riches and wealth. The longings were real. But now, they existed as a distant memory of a childhood, helpless in its misery. Back then, the pleasures had been elusive, like flowers on lofty trees—inviting but unattainable. He thought of his widowed mother and elder brother who had taken to tilling the land at a tender age. They had struggled to make both ends meet. Vararuchi was exposed to their back-breaking hardship, and was beset by troubling questions. If destiny had willed so much harshness on his simple innocent childhood, then surely its writ must be challenged, its influence reined in and vanquished. His days at the hermitage were preoccupied with this thought as he took his first lessons in learning. With a single-mindedness born of adversity, the young Vararuchi sought to overturn, to rewrite his destiny.

What then had passed since? What had become of those stirrings in this young mind? Indeed, as he uncovered new ground and liberated himself with knowledge, there seemed to set in a subtle disenchantment. It was as though the steel of his determination had lost its sheen somewhat. The passing away of his mother and his brother's loss shortly thereafter only pushed him further away from all earthly charms. The sense of futility, of a vision well lost, was complete. It had all been a childish fancy he would muse, on looking back. The divide between the rich and the poor, the attachment to worldly pursuits—he saw through these frailties in the human condition, deciphering the law of Nature at work. To reach the wellspring of Truth was now his sole aim. It was this that had spurred him on his journey. So much of pain, so much misery, had only strengthened his resolve. Still wet with the tears of his early years, the force within him remained an enduring one, abiding in its earnestness. All feeling of vengeance had disappeared. His was now a search devoid of conquest. It would be a testimonial, a beacon, for generations to come. Hopefully, someone, somewhere may make some good of it.

\*\*\*

A cool breeze caressed the young man's features in the stillness of the night. The leaves above swayed in a hum. The waters danced tranquilly. All was serene.

He awoke with a start. An agitated flapping of wings shattered his thoughts. He looked up. High above, on the branches of the banyan tree, a winged couple had made its home. Silhouetted eerily by the greyness of the night, they fluttered by their nest.

Vararuchi sensed something divine when he gazed at the birds. Weren't these beings endowed with foresight into the workings of destiny? Awakened from his thoughts, he sat prostate by the banyan tree. From his lips escaped a silent cry: 'Revered Gods of the wilderness, save me, save me.' The silent chant restored serenity to his troubled features. A passing breeze smoothed his countenance as he lay by the tree. The placid waters of the river shimmered in the darkness. Suddenly, the silence was broken by the sound of singing in the distance. A melodious song was being sung. The music seemed to meander dreamily from the heart of the thicket to where the young man lay.

He opened his eyes. A picture of completeness greeted him: the huge banyan with its leaves delicately dancing under the sky, the birds engrossed in each other in its branches above. The leaves hummed gently as they rustled in the night air. His eyes were drawn to the stars as they twinkled in the dark expanse. How differently they shone here—a lonesome, weary light here, a timid spark there. Strange, he mused, there was once a time when these ups and downs had moved him profoundly. He tilted his head for a better view.

Arundhati, Ashwati, Shukran, the Seven Maidens, Saturn… the names forming soundlessly on his lips. All of a sudden, as though reminded of something, he folded his hands and closed his eyes. A fervent prayer escaped his lips:

*Ahalya, Draupadi, Sita*
*Mandodari and Tara*
*With the thought of the maidens five*
*All sins are bade to fie.*

At that moment he heard a creaking sound. Startled, Vararuchi turned around. The temple that had appeared forlorn and deserted had flung its doors open. Heavy wooden planks weighed down with age swung noisily on rusted hinges. As he looked, there emerged from the darkness a bright flame from an oil lamp. The figure that held the lamp advanced slowly towards Vararuchi. A priest, bent with age, stood before him. The old man raised his lamp to see who was before him. The flickering glow illuminated the features of an upright young man standing with eyes lowered in respect. Long hair fell to his shoulders; the faint beginnings of manhood had darkened his countenance somewhat. His belongings and a wooden staff lay by the side. Standing by the riverbank thus, Vararuchi cut a handsome, if austere, figure of the young seeker that he was.

'I heard someone praying aloud,' the old man muttered as though to himself.

'It was me,' replied Vararuchi, 'chanting before lying down.'

'Aren't you a Brahmin?' interrupted the old man, noting the slender thread slung across the young man's chest.

'Yes.'

'And in this wilderness...' the old man's voice trailed questioningly.

'I am a wanderer who has stopped to take rest by the wayside. I'm on a quest to discover the eternal Truth.' Vararuchi spoke with the earnestness of the seeker.

'Will you have something to eat?'

'I've just had my supper.'

'Then perhaps you could come inside and keep warm,' the old man gestured to his little abode.

'It's so tranquil here in the open. One can watch the stars as they drift and eavesdrop on the conversation of birds above,' Vararuchi shied away from the old man's welcome.

The old man stood wondering, 'Drift of the stars, conversation of birds...' What was he hearing?

'These things hold meaning for me,' said Vararuchi. 'The heightened perception is the result of perseverance and penance at the feet of my master. These stars—,' Vararuchi continued, gesturing upwards, 'where they stand, where they go, the way they are aligned, their coming together, then moving apart—all interest me greatly. Under the tutelage of Aryabhatta I seek to learn this science. My journey leads to his centre of learning.'

The old man listened, unmoving, 'Why does one need to know all these?'

Leading the old man's gaze heavenward, Vararuchi explained, 'These stars you see above, they are more than shining bodies. They are celestial beings with infinite influence over all life on earth. Even as we speak, unseen forces are at work on us, around us. Invisible celestial rays, unheard waves of sound—these are the medium of their influence.' He declared boldly, 'I seek to uncover the secrets of Nature; my life is devoted to the cause.'

The old priest was nonplussed. Celestial rays, secrets of nature, and a cause, it seemed. Turning away, he quietly traced his steps homewards. His voice trailed into the night, '…the nights have been stormy, it might rain heavily. Come in, you can sleep inside.'

Vararuchi looked at the skies trustingly. 'Not at all, the skies are clear enough. Beneath the silvery stars, by the rhythm of the river and the leaves—no, no Sir, this is far too enchanting to forsake. Thank you, but I choose to sleep right here.'

The old man had paused briefly but now he walked on, the lamp by his side gently rocking in the darkness. Vararuchi heard the grating sound of the old door as the man shut himself in. The night resumed its vigil. Vararuchi lay resting by the banyan tree. The stillness of the night was broken by a song from above:

*'Heard you, my dear*
*Heard you, my dear*
*The young man yonder;*
*So prone to ponder*

*Of all things rife*
*Wishes to study life!'*

Vararuchi sat up startled. The clairvoyant messengers again! The male had spoken to the female, its voice mockingly derisive. The female replied, in a similar tone:

*'A study of life?*
*Come, that's a joke!*
*T'aint no science,*
*No great secret*
*In all its flavour,*
*One needs simply savour;*
*Such is life, such is life.'*

Her partner replied:

*'Truly spoken, my love,*
*Truly spoken.*
*Perhaps experience will teach him;*
*We bide our time, we bide our time.'*

Vararuchi listened keenly to the exchange. The birds had now ceased their chatter. The song that hung in the stillness of the night grew louder. The plaintive chorus quickened, rumbling in from the distance. But soon the rising hum slackened and the jungle hushed into silence, as though foretelling an arrival. Suddenly the cry of a newborn pierced the silent night air. The cry rent the wilderness as the night awoke to this sign of new life. Unnerved, Vararuchi sat up, his demeanour affected. At length he rose, walked up to the closed door of the little shrine, and knocked insistently.

'Oh holy one, are you listening?'

The door opened from within. The old man held up his lantern to the night. Standing framed by the doorway was the young monk. His face was pale and his eyes bloodshot. Gone was the assurance in his speech and manner so evident a little while ago. His face was etched with worry; he looked pleadingly at the priest. From beyond where he stood he heard the sharp cry of a newborn baby.

Amid the din, the old priest asked calmly, 'Do you want to come inside and sleep?'

'No...it's not that', stammered Vararuchi, 'this cry of the baby, here...at this time...' His voice trembled.

The priest continued, calm as ever, 'Not far from here are the dwellings of some poor people. You'd have heard them singing some time back. It's a time of thanksgiving for the people. Perhaps a child has been born to a couple.'

'Nothing to fear,' he added reassuringly, 'you could sleep inside if you want.'

Vararuchi regained his composure. Hastily declining the old man's welcome he mumbled, 'No, no it wasn't fear. I'm quite all right here. Just couldn't make sense of it. The night, the wilderness, the baby's cry...it all sounded so eerie. Very sorry for having troubled you, Sir.'

Without a word, the old man turned, closing the door behind him. Vararuchi returned to his spot by the tree. The baby's cries, which had quietened somewhat, now rose again, louder and louder. The cry echoed through the forest, destroying the stillness and peace of the night. Vararuchi felt very uncomfortable.

From above was heard the sing-song again:

*'Oh dear, oh dear,*
*Pitiful is this cry*
*That rings in the night*
*Without pause, without end.'*

Came the rejoinder from her companion:

*'It is a little girl that cries*
*In search of a mate*
*It is only natural,*
*The law of Nature.'*

The female's curiosity was aroused.

*'Mate, did you say?*
*Aha, is he hereabouts?'*

Vararuchi was intrigued beyond measure. The male's answer, however, would unsettle him:

*'The young man that lies beneath*
*That studies stars in the sky;*
*He is the one, he is the one,*
*He is the mate the child seeks.'*

Vararuchi's heart skipped a beat. What was he hearing? Surely the clairvoyant messengers were talking nonsense! He who had pledged himself to celibacy, who was devoted to seeking the Truth—to think that the future held such a possibility...Vararuchi was shaken.

The female spoke, doubtful:

*'Of lowly caste, in poverty bred,*
*That this poor girl would wed*
*A princely boy, of superior ken,*

*Isn't the match an unlikely one?'*
Her companion's reply was firm:
*'For sure, for sure,
It is ordained.
The writ of destiny
Awaits its unfolding.
The writ of destiny
Brooks no undoing.'*

Vararuchi sprang up and looked angrily upwards, from where the voices came. 'Never, never! The writ of destiny will never happen. It is I, Vararuchi, who says this. This will never happen,' he yelled.

Agitated, Vararuchi walked up and down, wringing his hands in sheer exasperation. At length his gait slackened as he quietened visibly. Looking all around in the darkness, as though searching for someone who would hear him, he declared at the top of his voice, 'Let this be heard, oh Lords of the cardinal directions, Mother Nature, Clairvoyant Messengers! I have heard my fate, my destiny. But I Vararuchi, am capable of rewriting my destiny... I will prove destiny wrong by my actions. Bear witness, divine forces, that Vararuchi shall not be turned back in his resolve, come what may.'

Speaking thus, he gathered his staff and belongings and disappeared into the night. Presently the skies darkened, the stars hid under heavy clouds and lightning flashed threateningly. A maddening wind tore through the heart of the forest, shaking trees in its wake. Thunder rent the night air as it began to pour heavily. In the midst of all this fury, the two birds held fast to the trembling branch of the banyan tree. The female clung close to her companion, trying to see where the young man had gone. Her heart heavy, in a quivering voice she asked:

*'Where goes he, my love*
*Where goes he?*
*So very angry he appeared to be,*
*Away from his mate-to-be.'*

Her mate scoffed:

*'The stars hold no secrets for him,*
*The rumbling clouds, this beating rain,*
*He understands them all, in the grain*
*Why he can even gauge,*
*The sing-song of our language.*
*But (sigh), vainglorious is he*
*(for) even the King waits on his words.*
*He is all set, it seems to me*
*To ruin his little mate-to-be.'*

The female was in tears.

*'Oh dear, oh dear,*
*That our conversation would so affect*
*The young man that goes afoot.*
*The rage that sits on his darkened brow*
*Bodes not well for the morrow.'*

The male spoke comfortingly:

*'The bad, the good and the sublime,*
*All lie in the womb of time;*

*In tandem with its mighty reach,*
*Ours alone to lend sight and speech.*
*What riches, what ironies lie in that realm,*
*Come my love, let's find out forthwith.'*

The birds took flight, their wings beating in unison, as though to the rhythm of a distant foreboding. With tragic precision they flew into the night like two arrows sprung from the sling of destiny. A creaking sound was heard as the temple doors swung open on their hinges. A bright flame danced uncertainly on its wick, in its darting glow could be seen the shadowy form of the aged priest. Insecure in the caring arc of his palm, the flame jerked wildly in the stormy night. Above the din of the beating rain and the furious wind, was heard the priest's cry, 'Oh traveller, won't you come inside? Oh traveller!'

His voice was lost in a deafening roar of thunder. As though with a vengeance, the wind tore through the thicket where the old man stood, snuffing out the cowering flame in one disdainful sweep. From deep in the forest came the sound of a terrible crash, as if a tree had fallen.

And the endless rain continued, unceasing...

# The Scholar's Devious Plot

Vararuchi strode farther and farther into the vast expanse of time. His quest took him from one school of learning to another, as the changing seasons wove their magic around him. In the splendid hues of the rainbow and in various fragrances they lavished themselves in his path. The changing air was picturesque. Drying autumnal leaves swirled around him in hazy circles even as the woods darkened in the arid air. Now and then the eye was tricked by the sight of a dizzying mirage. With the rains came the rainbow, and fresh young buds sprung up everywhere to welcome the showers. And then it was spring, laden with blossoms on the waters. The autumn woods trembled and leaves dropped silently to earth, even as a summer sped through the scorching heat in search of a cool glade. Unaffected by the changing colours and moods of nature, Vararuchi continued on his journey. Only his body showed some signs of the passing time; his determination and mind remained fixed. His education was boundless, encompassing every aspect of knowledge. He unravelled the mysteries of stars, planets, and astral bodies at the legendary Aryabhatta's school of astrology. His experiments at the revered Kanaadan's centre of learning led to an understanding of the very nature of this earth. He studied Ayurveda at the feet of the pioneering masters Charaka and Susruta. Discourses and debates under the tutelage of Brihaspati and Vachaspati invigorated his intellect and appetite for knowledge. In the arts, Mammadabhatta awakened him to a critical appreciation of literature and its principles. His instinct for language was sharpened by discourse and exchange at Kundakan's. At the school of Chaarvakku, a world of physical sciences opened up new frontiers in Vararuchi's thirst for knowledge.

Unending and laborious was his thirst to unravel the mystery of life, the secrets of joy and sorrow... His research went into every aspect of human understanding to discover the essence of life. It was a daunting task that required grit, concentration and enduring great tribulation. Throughout these seventeen years of immense struggle his mind was restless and insecure. Almost every day after a hard day's work, his soul was disturbed by the helpless cry of the little girl.

However much he tried to forget he could not. From somewhere in the recesses of his memory, there echoed the cry, disquieting in its fervour, unsettling in its stillness. The helpless cry of a poor, newborn girl child. Try as he might, the episode remained unforgotten, undiminished. Memory shone through attempts to conceal it, at justifications in the name of wisdom, duty or purpose. The passage of time would only heighten the ghastliness of the deed. In the hours after his study, as he sought a moment's rest, the memory would come unbidden, disturbing his peace and equanimity. Poor, helpless child; his conscience was laden with guilt.

What meanness, trying to kill a poor child! Could a scholar, a man of wisdom, stoop to such a lowly act? But then, his intellect reasoned, one can't sum it up all that simply. What if you realized the truth of my intentions? If you knew that the child held the seed of a foreboding—one that could shake the very foundations of faith, of customs and tradition? You cannot be so harsh if you could only foresee the upheavals to happen, were the prophecy to come true. A Brahmin boy with a girl from a lowly caste? Unthinkable! Do I seem mean and self-centred? Is it unbecoming to think so? But am I not to look after my interests? And what right has another to hinder my ambitions?

But this was the voice of cultivated thought and cold reason. Confined to its quest, its morality was a bounded one. If this was all that mattered, what was the trepidation that he felt, as though of a clamouring at the walls? Into the stronghold of his convictions something had wormed its way in—unheeding, unbidden. It was indifferent to argument, reasoning, and loud assertions of right and wrong. Though it was unassuming, rather weak in stature, an all-too-human sentiment, remorse at the wrongdoing had pervaded deep within him. He couldn't wish the innocent voices away; nor could he reason with them, for they passed unchallenged— the underdogs of justice. It was as though his defences were breached, not in combat but rather by a foregone conclusion.

In the stillness of his nights, the pleas grew loud and shrill, shattering his calm and tearing at his very being. Poor, helpless child.

'Vararuchi!' a voice reprimanded him. 'There's an ebbing in your penance, a slackening in your quest. Are you a weakling that you cry like this?'

Truth be told, beneath the resolute young man he now appeared to be, there was a struggling child, with a trembling heart. From childhood his mother had been an abiding influence on him. The memory of her love overcame him.

'Vararuchi!'

The tired voice of his brother resounded in his memory. Vararuchi winced. His brother had never known a moment's rest and had borne great hardships—all for him, so that his younger brother might become a man of learning, a great man. And what had come about in the wake of it all? The years of unremitting toil had taken their toll. Vararuchi remembered only too well the hastily scrawled note his brother had left behind:

*My dear child,*

*Listen carefully and do not be troubled by what I'm going to say. Circumstances make it difficult for me to stay here any longer. While I can I'll cross the border and escape to Nepal. Far away from everything we know, I hope to find protection there.*

*But don't you worry. Your aspirations lie in the realm of learning, of wisdom. And there'll be none happier than me to see you become a scholar. As for me, I'm a sinner. Your coming with me shall only wreck your dreams.*

*And that shall not be. The world we've come into has been a harsh one and our life until now has been a bitter experience. From the ashes of our humble beginnings you should rise tall. You are blessed with superior intellect and reasoning, and you alone can make all our dreams come true.*

*Pardon me for leaving you like this. You know well there's no one I care for more than you in this whole world. Though from afar, your brother awaits news of your rise to fame and fortune. And I certainly wouldn't wish to darken your glorious endeavour with the shadow of my presence.*

*In the prospect of us meeting sometime, somewhere, in happier times.,*

*I remain,*

*Your loving brother.*

Sharp, rushed scribbles on the rough palm leaf. That was the last he had heard of his brother. And he had chanced upon the note much too late, Vararuchi thought bitterly. It was on the auspicious night of the new moon, marked by fasting, that he had paid a visit home. The premises looked long deserted, like a home abandoned in flight. There, on the porch by the gate lay a sheaf of leaves loosely tied together: his brother's farewell note.

Somewhere along the way, the momentous little note was forgotten. But the lines remained, etched in his memory. What desperation had driven his brother to go away? Stories abounded. One he had heard later shook him; he couldn't believe that his brother had been driven to such an act. Of a theft...the royal gold at the temple where his brother had served...but that couldn't be. Why would he ever do something like that? Could he have committed such a crime, perhaps, on account of his younger brother's education? Vararuchi receiving the education he had always wanted meant, of course, fees, offerings to the Master—so many expenses. Coming to think of it, Vararuchi had always been provided for.

'...*Circumstances make it difficult for me to stay here any longer.*' Indeed, he could well imagine.

That was the last he had heard of his brother. He did not know what fate had met him since. The road to Nepal was rife with treacherous mountain passes; the forests there were home to wild beasts. Could it be, Vararuchi shuddered but then dismissed the thought, of cannibals that inhabited those jungles? An overwhelming sadness came over Vararuchi. Looking back, his life had been an endless saga of hardships, a bitter childhood borne on poverty, hunger, need. Mother, father, brother—everyone beloved to him—had succumbed to the harshness of fate.

***

But was that a trace of weariness creeping over his resolute features? No, that would never be. Vararuchi strode on, unflinching; not a hint of vulnerability. After all these years, he had quite forgotten those bleak times. The coldness that now masked his countenance betrayed none of those early stirrings of ambition, overcoming, and vengeance. The transformation was near complete, almost convincing.

Yet, he hadn't had the courage to carry out a killing in cold blood. On that fateful night, he had been beside himself with vexation. All through the driving rain and wind, he had reasoned endlessly with himself. The birds, he knew well, were endowed with divine foresight. What they spoke was as irrefutable as destiny itself. But they had predicted a fate that would translate across generations, a sentence that would wreak its consequences unseeing, unknowing. But for a man who lived by his actions what meaning did destiny hold? The sciences, the school of rational thought held that all hindrances in the path of action and rightful conduct be set aside, eliminated. All this reasoning, however justified, could not bring Vararuchi to commit the dastardly act himself, even though fulfilling it was central to his journey. In his frenzied mind he remembered the King's parting words:

'Vararuchi, whatever be your need, whenever you choose to, come back to me. You are always welcome.'

An idea had formed in his head: why not make it a royal decree to have the child executed in the interests of the state? Surely the King would not refute the words of a wise man. Stepping into the royal court once more, Vararuchi was greeted in awe by the King.

'Young man, I presume that you are in the course of your wanderings. So what brings you here to brighten our palace?'

But his manner changed as he noted Vararuchi's appearance. Pale and dishevelled, the Vararuchi that stood before him was a far cry from the confident, young man who had mesmerized his court....Was this the young man who had walked out on the royal seat of honour? He looked defeated, exhausted. Concerned, the King asked, 'What has happened, O revered one? All is well I hope. Or does your darkened brow hint of a foreboding?'

Sullen, Vararuchi replied, 'You are right, my Lord. I bring uneasy tidings. An evil one has been born in your kingdom. It endangers the prosperity of the state and casts a shadow over your years in glory, my Lord.'

Disbelieving, the King looked on as Vararuchi continued, 'By the banks of the Shipra River, not far from its origins, is a Mahakala Temple. Close by, in a hutment of the lowly castes, a girl child has been born...' Vararuchi paused for effect, 'under the sign of the Ashveena Panchami. It is an evil birth that will be ominous for your reign, my Lord. If unchecked, it could spell doom for your rule and the kingdom.'

The King was shocked. The words of the prodigious scholar had an unmistakable ring of a foretelling. Desperately, he asked, 'Is there a way out, young sir?'

As though anticipating the question, Vararuchi replied, 'Why yes, my Lord. It is to be nipped in the bud.' His look and gesture left no room for doubt as to the intended course of action.

The King was aghast. 'Vararuchi, what are you suggesting? Killing an infant, a girl child at that! Surely it is the most wretched of sins. For generations to come, the curse of such an act would be visited on us. No, no, we cannot do that.'

At the moment of reckoning, while the King had waited on his words, Vararuchi had spoken unthinkingly. Forgotten for a moment was all intellect, all sense of right and wrong, all his gathered wisdom. He had spoken in the voice of fear and vengeance—undisguised, unmasked. Gathering himself, Vararuchi replied, 'Far be it, my Lord, for me to even suggest such a heinous act. The sacred texts do, however, suggest a recourse. What is suggested is a casting away of the child in a raft of plantain leaves,' he continued evenly, 'with a thorn impaled on its forehead. To the accompaniment, of course, of ritual and alms to the poor. To the land and its people this would be an act of cleansing.'

And so it was to be. At once the palace pundits and courtiers proceeded to act upon the young man's words. Vararuchi himself was at the helm of the rituals, gravely presiding over an occasion marked with much ceremonial fervour and chanting. It was, to all appearances, an act of cleansing for the kingdom and its people.

It was late evening when the rituals drew to a close. The act completed, Vararuchi took a dip in the waters. His wish was fulfilled, his conscience sanctified. In the fading light he retraced his steps. The riverbank was desolate. A lone Kadamba tree stood silhouetted against the evening sky. All of a sudden, the picturesque silence was broken. He heard a flutter, as though a flapping of wings overhead. Looking up, Vararuchi started. Rising from the stricken branches, their wings blurring in an agitated flapping were two birds.

They hovered above the waves, moving to the distant horizon. Beneath them, the river carried the forsaken raft in a dizzying downswing. Amid the swirling waters the shrill cry of the grieving, abandoned child could be heard. Vararuchi could barely conceal his triumph. Poor birds, what had come of their foretelling, he thought vainly. Yet, it was true that his elation was fraught with unease. The shrill cry pierced his being, a thorn that would prick at him for the years to come in his quest. The cry also brought back a memory of the moment—the little helpless body writhing in torment as the thorn dug deeper into her scalp. The cries now grew distant as the little boat drifted further and further away. The waves played havoc with it, tossing it here and there, until at last they seemed like echoes from the infernal depths of the river.

In his disturbed conscience, the echoes resounded, destroying his peace of mind, robbing him of quiet. Often he would try to justify himself: hadn't he acted in good faith, in keeping with the approved rites of passage in a four-tiered society—as a devout Brahmin on whom was incumbent the sixteen holy strictures? So, how was he wrong? An inner voice spoke up: 'But wasn't there a vested interest in the act? To serve your ends you faked your intentions at the King's court. The act of bringing order to the state was unmistakably tinged with self-interest and fraud. Do you call that righteousness?'

'Self-interest? Fraud? What if the foretelling of the birds were allowed to come true? The destruction of ritual, erosion of values, and resulting upheaval of society would have spelt doom for the King and the state. My intervention has only served to avert what would certainly have been a disaster. And there hasn't been the slightest sign of dissent either. In a kingdom of peace-loving, God-fearing people, the act hasn't so much as raised an eyebrow. Like any other ritual ordained by the gods, the people have taken to it peacefully, willingly submitting to the writ of tradition. Why, there hasn't been a murmur from the people at the hutment even!

But yet, but yet. The unease continued, the pinpricks of a guilty conscience. Or could it be something even more terrible; the sum of all his fears: the great Vararuchi's covert attempt to thwart an innocent life at birth would come to light.

Higher and higher into the realms of knowledge Vararuchi ventured, in pilgrimage from one hermitage to the other, moving from one centre of learning to another. But do what he might, the sense of something missing remained. Peace of mind and contentment were to elude him forever. Of what use then was all his learning if it could not bring him the simple, unalloyed pleasure of being? And what good was a life bereft of peace and contentment? In vain did he search for an answer, knocking at the doors of eminent masters and wise men.

'All my learning, my erudition, has come undone because of this...The truth of my inquiry remains imprisoned, hopelessly unyielding. Pray show me the key that I may pry it open for a glimpse, so that a grain of peace might light my weary soul.'

But little did the masters know of Vararuchi's predicament. The key lay in the dark recesses of his conscience, a conscience that was closed to understanding and human sentiment. Unknowing, they advised, 'Vararuchi, too much of work and wandering have made your body and soul weary. Your mind is overwrought. A stay at the hermitage of Dhanvantari would do you a world of good. Go, son, rejuvenate yourself, come back refreshed and with renewed vigour for the good life.'

So it was that Vararuchi found himself at the doorstep of Sage Dhanvantari, physician sage seasoned in mind-body remedies, scholarly and wise with years of experience.

# The Long Walk of the Agnostic

The glacial peaks of the Himalayas stood tall and imposing. Within its folds lay the picturesque landscape of the valley. From its peaks the Saugandhika River flowed merrily. Clumps of deodars dotted the embankment. In their shade by the water's edge lay a spread of low, thatch-roofed dwellings: the hermitage of Sage Dhanvantari. From inside could be heard a murmur of prayers in chanting, the whisper of lips moving soundlessly in unison. The rigour of learning and exercise resounded in the air by the riverbank. White clouds of smoke rose from the ritual chambers. The air was laden with the mingled fragrances of locally plucked and indigenous herbs. Around the classrooms and prayer halls, and throughout the valley, saffron flowers blossomed, marking the boundaries of the hermitage. The crystal mountain peaks caught the first rays of the sunlight, bathing the surroundings in a blinding light.

A tall and handsome, though haggard looking, young man ascended the steps to the entrance of the hermitage. At the gates he was met by a hermit, a disciple of the Sage. The unkempt hair and shabby appearance of the bearded youth couldn't disguise the unmistakable air of scholarliness that permeated from within him. The disciple bowed low in welcome.

'The wise Brahmin Vararuchi, unless I'm mistaken? Welcome Sir, to our humble abode.'

Vararuchi was taken aback. How was he recognized here? Had someone informed them of his coming?

Sensing his disbelief, the young hermit explained, 'Your fame is far reaching, your prowess legendary; O revered. Our master has sent word of your coming and for us to make all arrangements for your stay here.'

Still dazed by the foresight of Sage Dhanvantari, Vararuchi faltered.'I'm dizzy with exhaustion. May I have an audience with His Holiness now?'

Concerned, the disciple answered, 'It is the fifth day of the month of Ashweena, you might well know, wise one. An inauspicious coming together of the planets, a time of great consternation. Our master is occupied; rituals and meditation are underway to ward off the evil eye. As soon as they're over, you may see him.'

The month of Ashweena, an inauspicious union? Where had he heard that before? Borne on the waters of a distant memory, an image came knocking at his consciousness. He remembered a tiny newborn child writhing in agony, hurtling down the depths of the river to its ill-fated end. From the depths of his forgetting, there echoed a cry. The cry tore at his insides, breaking loose the long-fastened doors of his conscience. He shuddered, and mumbled faintly, 'I'm tired, I'm done...'

His weariness must have been evident, for the disciple sprang to his feet at the words. A strong pair of arms supported Vararuchi and led him gently inside. The comforts of a special chamber for visitors of distinction awaited him. When he came to himself, the soft deerskin mattress felt warm and comforting to his back. A cool air caressed his senses. He opened his eyes. A line of bamboo rafters beneath the thatched roof met his gaze. Was it early morning or the fading evening light? And what had become of time, which flowed ceaselessly from the shroud of yesterday to the light of today and from there to the darkness of the morrow? And the waves that danced in its stream? All was still, unmoving. Passing moments dropped soundlessly on the placid waters. Yet, not a ripple disturbed the surface.

Where was he? What had happened? He drifted uncontrollably into unconsciousness. Then with an effort, his heavy eyelids fluttered open. A golden twilight stole through the chinks in the rustling leaves by the window. He saw great clouds gliding gently across the sky. Under the fading glow of the evening, everyone was returning home: birds darted back to their nests, a shepherd sounded the call of return and his herd fell into a bustling pitter-patter as they trod homeward. Still in a reverie lay Vararuchi, his mind leading him along a familiar, long-forgotten path. It was the river of his childhood, a thin stream that wound its way through the village. By its banks, near the village shrine, stood a house—a crumbling porch rather, a shelter that was home. A fragrance of dahlias wafted through the years; he could see them bright and blossoming in the yard facing the steps.

Wasn't it Mother that stood before him? Forehead creased in worry, cheeks sunken and frail in body, it was indeed his mother. Brother too was close behind, their faces etched with anxiety. Vararuchi cried out fearfully, 'Mother, what is it, what's happening to me?'

A voice spoke reassuringly, 'Nothing to fret, wise one. The years of work and travel have worn you out a little. Our master had come by just a while ago.'

The unexpected remark startled him. Seated by the bedside, Vararuchi realized, was a young hermit. Vararuchi recognized him as the disciple he had met at the gates. He gathered himself. It was the first time that he had fallen this ill and needed care and attention. Had he been looked after like this before?

The disciple's words interrupted his thoughts. 'For a while you had us all worried. But then our master allayed our fears. He has pronounced it as a case of exhaustion brought about by great stress to the body and mind.' He hastened to add, 'Nothing that a little relaxation can't cure. Tomorrow, the eighth day of the month, marks the last day of rituals. Our master shall visit you in the morning.'

The eighth! Vararuchi recollected dimly that his coming had coincided with a coming together of the planets. Yes, it had been the fifth day of the month of Ashweena. Three days had passed since his arrival!

'Vararuchi!' It was a familiar voice that reproached him. 'Are you getting so old that your body, your intellect fails you so? What has come of your quest, the vows you undertook to fulfil?'

His lips moved in a silent utterance.

*Frail of heart and spirit feeble,*
*Ill does it suit a man of mettle;*
*Mighty warrior it is unbecoming,*
*Banish the thought, arise unflinching.*

Whose words were these? From the blur of his past the lines echoed. The idyllic picture of a village—a river winding through it, a shrine by its edge, and a crumbling, broken shelter that was home—rose in his mind again. One day at school, in the middle of classes, he had been summoned home urgently. Innocent, unknowing, he had started on the way. His heart sank as he climbed the steps to the porch. It was the moment of truth. His mother was no more. He remembered not having wept at the time. The shock had been greater. The loss of a mother who had scrounged for a living by working at Brahmin households in the village, for whom happiness, comfort, and the luxuries of life had meant little in a lifetime of dreary labour. It was for her that he had set out to conquer so many worlds. If his brother could not, it was his duty to wrest this life into his own hands and win everything, all for her. And now with her loss, his towering ambition had suddenly come apart. Nothing mattered any longer.

Long after the funeral rites were complete he had remained indoors; sullen, indifferent and detached from the comings and goings around him. As dawn broke on the last day of abstinence he confronted his brother with a decision: 'I shall not be going to school anymore.'

His brother was silent. Though a good ten years separated them, they had always been friends first, comrades-in-arms who had endured the unevenness of the times together. He felt that his brother approved of his decision. Was it relief at being spared the expense of a continuing education? As a small-time help to the priest of the temple his earnings were meagre; they were always hard-pressed to make ends meet. And now with the passing away of Mother, perhaps the thought had rankled.

The day wore on, vague and indecisive. The twilight hour marked the end of the day's rituals at the temple. The deities were laid to rest and offerings distributed. It was night when his brother returned home. He appeared to have made up his mind.

'You have to go, my dearest brother. You need to complete your education.' He continued, 'Life has been unfair to us. What wrong had our mother done to suffer so in her life? What is the meaning of our daily struggles? With gritted teeth and fists clenched, we've borne so many hardships together. But,' he paused, his eyes shining with grim determination, 'not any more, not if we can help it. The time has come to challenge the past. One of us must stand up and be counted among the victorious and the successful.'

And his brother recited Lord Krishna's advice to Arjuna who stood overcome at the battleground:

*Frail of heart and spirit feeble,*
*Ill does it suit a man of mettle;*
*Mighty warrior it is unbecoming,*
*Banish the thought, arise unflinching.*

It was the beginning of his acquaintance with the Bhagavad Gita. The lines touched him and would remain etched in his mind forever. The lines inspired him at school and spurred him in competition among classmates. They lent solace at the loss of a dear brother. And on an ill-fated night, after a shattering revelation, as he walked helpless and dejected, the words had shone, fierce and enlightening, a beacon unto his despairing soul. Now, at this moment of uncertainty, his brother's lesson echoed.

*…Mighty warrior it is unbecoming,*
*Banish the thought, arise unflinching.*

Where would Brother be? It was now twenty-six years since they had met. He had then been in his third year of tutelage. Vararuchi threw his head back in recollection. He tried to fix his brother in his memory but could not. After all these years would they recognize each other? Maybe they would pass each other unknowingly, as ships in the darkness of the night. His mind lingered on an image—a tall, thinning figure, fair and handsome: a brother who had been older than his years, loving and protective of him. Born and bred in poverty, they were set adrift in time like dry leaves in the arid air. They fluttered uncertainly, rustling, now blown hither and thither as the passing draught caught them unawares. Hapless and unmoored, they were swept by the gusts of time, amid thorns, into forgotten crevices. Which way would the merciless wind blow next?

His mind reverted to the unforgettable day of their parting, and the missing royal gold at the temple where his brother had served. The upheaval in the wake of the discovery had tainted their names forever. His brother's abrupt flight—was it to spare ignominy to the family, or was it simply bound to happen, so that Vararuchi might pursue the education he had always wanted? He grew dizzy at the thought. No, he didn't want to know the answers any more. Whichever way he looked at it, there was no escaping the remorse he felt. Poor brother, his intentions had been true, after all.

'There you go again, feeble heart!'

A voice he recognized as his brother's reproached him. Vararuchi quickly gathered his bearings. But no, if only his brother knew of the hardy man his timid little one had grown into, a man who lived by the wisdom of the Gita: *Arise, awake, and quell the enemy!* Who had discovered lofty truths along the way; that in the course of evolution, creation and destruction go hand in hand. Who had used this reasoning to justify a momentous act, one he would have no misgivings about—sentencing a girl child to an untimely end.

Brother would approve. Memory was no longer an oppressive thing, all frailty had been stamped out. For a fleeting moment Vararuchi sensed an elation; a triumph over the tribulations that had dogged him his entire life… The moment was precious—for it was soon to pass. Doubt and misgivings reclaimed their possession of his overwrought mind. True, he had become free of the shackles that once chained him; but the greying thin cobwebs of a memory bound him yet. It had been easy to splinter great rocks to dust. But the difficulty lay in caressing and plucking the tender petals of a flower. Therein lay a reality that was at once simple and profound. Beyond wisdom, beyond seeking, beyond all becoming. In this fragrant hearth throbbed a life; in all its vitality, a beauty that was everlasting. And he had dared to tread on this sacred ground.

'Oh! What a misadventure this has been! A tale gone awry at the bend. From where has this terrible ache, a venomous thorn, pierced my being. A disquiet has crept into my learning. This cry of a little child has shattered my peace of mind; it makes me faint.'

A despairing Vararuchi fell face down, arms stretched in fervent prayer: 'O Master, give me peace. Bring me back to the path of action.'

A hand caressed his forehead, the touch light and refreshing. Vararuchi opened his eyes. A pair of luminous, compassionate eyes looked out of a kind, smiling countenance. The wise Dhanvantari, physician and sage seasoned in mind-body remedies. Reaching out, he grasped Vararuchi's extended hands cupped in prayer.

'Arise, Vararuchi, nothing's the matter. You are perfectly all right.'

Vararuchi stammered, 'But then…'

The Sage spoke, reassuring: 'As one who has chosen the path of Truth, your predicament is only natural. For it is a long and arduous journey, with many a hardship along the way.'

The Sage's words had a rejuvenating effect. Already, weariness and exhaustion were beginning to fade away. In silence they walked towards the Master's chamber in the hermitage. Visibly relaxed, Vararuchi was nevertheless nonplussed at the change the encounter had wrought in him.

'How do I explain the quiet command with which this man has so effortlessly soothed my nerves?'

Once inside, the Sage bade Vararuchi to sit on the wooden seat meant for students. Vararuchi heard himself questioning the Sage.

'If I may ask, Sir, how did you divine of my seeking?'

The Sage replied, 'Your face is lit with a glow. The radiance of the seeker sits unmistakably on your countenance. May the gods bless you in your quest.'

Vararuchi hesitated then asked, 'But wise one, if you would pardon my saying so, wouldn't my success mean a defeat in your seeking? Aren't our paths so totally at odds with each other—that if one succeeds, it will necessarily be at the cost of the other?'

The Sage replied without hesitation, 'Both lead to the Truth. In its fulfilment our two paths can equally succeed.'

Vararuchi was not convinced. Candidly, he declared, 'I do not believe in a destiny ordained by birth. I have no faith in any form of organized religion whatsoever. My beliefs are grounded in reason, in science, in logic and rational thinking. Naturally, my analysis of all things in the universe stands the test of reasoning. All allusions to destiny and to fate become invalid, immaterial.'

Sage Dhanvantari spoke benevolently. 'For every writ that is ordained, you'll find a thousand non-believers up in arms against its proclamation. But if you observe carefully, the act of rebellion too has been foretold. And so, you have a single writ that has set a thousand others resonating in its wake. Indeed, you'd be wasting your energies in putting out these endless, raging fires.'

Vararuchi countered, 'In the advancement of all creation, destruction is inevitable, essential even.' He was regaining the quicksilver intellect that had won him the exalted seat at the king's court.

Sage Dhanvantari was thoughtful for a moment. 'What if the destruction is ill-intentioned? If it results in the helpless and poor being crushed in the name of advancement? The perishing of all plants and animals, little helpless children even?'

All the colour ran out of Vararuchi's face. Turning his head, he cocked an ear to the wind. The cries of a hapless girl child echoed in his ears. He trembled. The Sage's benediction has found its mark; a wound had opened afresh.

Vararuchi hung his head as the Sage continued: 'The mountains, the river, the trees, stars in the sky—are they merely objects that exist to satisfy a physical need? Look closely, you'll find all elements endowed with a life of their own, each with a voice, an emotion, a rightful place on this divine earth. The rich tapestry of nature is at once simple and tantalizing. In order to fathom the unfathomable, one needs a compassionate heart, one that can temper cold logic with intuition and experience. A tenderness would then suffuse your reasoning, no longer would it be coarse and dispassionate. In that enlightened realm of understanding, the worldly and the sublime would meld into a harmonious whole.'

His gift for repartee had deserted Vararuchi. He was once more a small boy overcome with emotion. He trembled inwardly, as though guilty of an unpardonable sin. His face was crestfallen. Sage Dhanwantari laid a consoling hand on his head.

The skies had begun to darken. The twilight was lit with the colours and moods of a late evening. Suddenly, the air was rent with the sound of a hundred bells ringing. From the meditation chambers rose the fervent strains of a prayer. In the rich tapestry of the song was interwoven every emotion. Hope and despair mingled in equal measure. It conjured visions of flowering paddy fields and stretching farmlands of golden corn. The sun had set. Over the song, one could catch the tired moan of oxen at the plough. The endearing laughter of children at play coursed through the song. And as lovers sought refuge in the forgiving darkness, a murmur of tender nothings echoed in the air.

Vararuchi was immersed in prayer. Eyes closed, he found himself reminiscing on his childhood years. In a trance, the fervent lines led him to a momentous discovery.

*Oh everlasting Truth,*
*All beings in the universe seek you,*
*meditate upon your presence;*
*Yet, the pursuit of happiness only breeds*
*endless conflict and sorrow in its wake.*
*The source of all seeking, oh divine Truth,*
*Give us also the compassion*
*to resolve this predicament.*
*And therein, the path to realizing you.*

The prayer had ended, the bells stopped clanging and the last of its echoes faded into silence. Vararuchi was speechless. Deep inside, he felt the touch of something infinitely tender. It was as though a wellspring of compassion had risen in his world of science and reasoning. His eyes glazed with a rare understanding.

Sage Dhanvantari rose, gazing steadily at the light in the young man's eyes. Vararuchi followed, rising to clasp the Master's outstretched hands. Each man was on the path of seeking. They might well have been travellers to the same destination. 'But,' cautioned the Sage to Vararuchi in parting, 'It is in our minds, our inside selves, that the answers lie. There, in the world of our consciousness, are the clues to be sought, the mysteries to be unravelled. Compassion, faith, and humility are the wheels that move this quest. It is for us to see that their movement is unending, unabated, forever.'

Vararuchi stood unblinking and poised, listening as the great man spelt out his wisdom. He fell at the Master's feet and sought his blessings. Master and disciple bade goodbye; it was now time for Vararuchi to move on.

It was a new Vararuchi who left the hermitage of Dhanvantari. Gone was the complacence and arrogance that had marked his personality. He clothed the naked, comforted the needy, and guided the wretched. Amid students in discourse he was at his humblest. Little things he had never known existed now caught his attention and delighted him endlessly. His eyes opened out to nature in all its pristine glory. And to think that he had spent his time so far in analysis, in examination of a beauty that was beyond measure, a truth too profound for words. In light of the new-found revelation, Vararuchi could not but look back with unease at his past glories. The little triumphs, the forgotten attainments—all seemed trivial, a realization only in part, an understanding bereft of wholeness. The Truth he had so clinically dissected; had he as much as paused to gaze in wonderment at its beauty? His learning, his erudition had been simply accumulative. Would they have measured up in the laboratory of real life?

And life, in all its richness, now stood before him, revealed. No longer was he indifferent to the changing colours and moods of nature. In the murmur of a brook, in the call of birds at twilight, in the unmoving tranquillity of the mountains, he discovered a tenderness that had eluded him so far. At the outskirts of towns, the countryside opened out to endless life and vitality. Golden fields of corn whispered gaily in the wafting wind. Here and there, tender stems wilted in the scorching sun. The earth was an enchanting mosaic as the trees rained flowers from above. At night, showers of a different kind left him drenched. All around nature beckoned invitingly.

Further and further into the vast expanse of time strode Vararuchi in his quest. The path less-travelled gave way at places to wide open roads and bustling towns. At times a bend in the road threw open an astonishing change of scene. In the wave of a hand, the busy thoroughfare gave way to the hinterland. The countryside opened in a rolling meadow of green, little rivulets coursed by his path.

As night fell, Vararuchi found himself in a tiny village by a river. Weary with exhaustion, he rested by a tree that stood on its banks. The night air was soothing. Before him the river descended in a roaring cascade. As the waters thundered into a descent, its foam sparkled in the darkness and moistened the air with a million droplets of water. He rested, relieved. A good night's sleep is what I need, he said to himself. By the light of early morning his journey would resume. He could reach the hermitage of Sage Shaaradwatam by nightfall. Shaaradwatam was well known for his explorations of space and time.

The plans for the next day gently eased from his thoughts. Sleep had only just begun to reclaim him when he heard a flutter overhead. He looked up, eyes half-closed in slumber. A dim recollection swung in hazily from a time long gone. Now nearing, now ebbing, a memory came to him uncertainly in half-sleep. Presently, the mist cleared: the

Shipra River at its origin, a shrine of the Mahakala temple by its banks...and indictment. He understood. It was the same river, now cascading at its confluence. The birds would be keeping time, he mused. Strange that he could observe them disaffectedly now. The Vararuchi of old would have been touched to the quick, angered at the mere suggestion of an ordaining. Poor birds, was all he could feel now. Why, he had uprooted their very foundations of destiny, of time, the basis of all reckoning.

Still lying down, he clapped his hands and called out into the darkness. His voice was tinged with more than a hint of sarcasm: 'Move on, you poor desolate ones! Fly away, poor unmoored souls! To the beginnings of the river, to the threshold of a divinity by its bank, so that you may beguile innocent wayfarers with treacherous tales of writ and prophecy. Move on, hapless souls!'

As though in response, like obedient children, they rose from the branches of the tree and vanished into the night. The sight brought a contemptuous smile to the young man's lips. They would have finally understood, though late, of the force that was Vararuchi—of its might that could quell, of its prowess that could overturn the workings of destiny even.

Still smiling, the young man drifted into a deep, contented sleep. The cool breeze caressed his features; and his face was peaceful as he slept by the riverbank.

# A Providential Sighting

Dawn had begun to break in the forest. The sky was awash in grey, a tint of silver at the edges as the first rays of the sun stole through the sombre expanse. A twitter of birds rang in the air; the river hummed perennially in the background. Somewhere in the distance a rooster cackled a call of awakening, signalling the arrival of a new day. Vararuchi opened his eyes. He lay curled by the riverbank, the seduction of a half-awakening lulled him back to sleep. 'To rise when the crow caws,' he said to himself.

A voice called out to him. Vararuchi opened his eyes. An old man dressed all in white stood before him. Bent with age, the weight of years sat markedly on his mane of white hair and a greying beard. Sandal paste and vermilion smeared on his forehead, he had the unmistakable air of a pious Brahmin, a Vaishnavite. He looked intently at the young man who lay by the foot of the tree. Vararuchi got to his feet and faced the stranger respectfully. He gazed at the old man enquiringly.

Presently the old man spoke. 'Where the river ends, by the quenching of the cascade, is a little shrine of worship. I am the priest there. My abode is also nearby.' He continued, 'Today marks the ninth day of the month of Karthika, with ceremonies and fasting in its wake. We are to partake of our meals only after the ritual initiation by a guest and granting of alms.'

He paused. 'It was my daughter who, after a dip in the river, brought me news of a young man she saw by the riverbank. Would you be my guest and grace our dwelling with your presence at this auspicious moment?' the old man entreated humbly. His face shone with the serenity of the believer. A steadfast pursuit of holiness had imbued his countenance with grace.

Vararuchi looked at him silently. Inwardly, he balked at the suggestion. A ritual initiation by a guest! A granting of alms! He had never been one to believe in these confounded practices. Why, these were simply religious escapades propagated by the people of his community so that they might make merry at the expense of another. To Vararuchi, whose religion was founded on rightful action, this was unthinkable; an end that hardly justified the means.

A sharp retort to the old man's request was at the tip of his tongue, but he paused. The pause was momentous, for it held the ache of a tumultuous coming of age for the young man. Not so long ago, his reply would have stung the listener in its offending frankness. He would have scorned any offer of alms, any gesture or overture to propitiate in the name of religion. Perhaps, if the old man had heard of Vararuchi, he would have never made such a suggestion. The erudite but vainglorious scholar would have more than lived up to his reputation not too long ago.

But the revelation at Sage Dhanwantari's hermitage had changed him forever. The Vararuchi that confronted the old man was a far cry from the brash, upstart pundit of old. He was now compassion personified, a man truly enlightened, mellowed by the passing of time, who strove to reconcile the seemingly tenuous opposites in his nature: an incisive, investigative temperament with a human, compassionate touch. Oh, what wounds his learning had wrought, no less the insights the wounds themselves had awoken. Perhaps that explained his unease at refusing the offer; the thought that he might hurt an old man pricked him. But would Vararuchi ever succumb to a stranger's whim at the cost of a conviction he held dear? In the end, it was the devious mind of the prodigious scholar that came to his rescue. He would accede of course, but in a manner that the old man would by himself secede.

Smugly he connived, 'It would indeed be unpardonable if I were to refuse the offer, Sir. And so, I shall come with you.' Vararuchi nodded reassuringly before adding, 'I have, however, a few conditions before I may indulge your request.'

The old man hesitated; he scarce knew what to expect of this Brahmin youth. 'What demands might they be?' he thought searchingly. 'Perhaps,' he thought consolingly, 'the man was a Shaivite, which simply meant a change in the course of rituals. Or perhaps, they didn't see eye to eye on the sacred texts each followed. And that would mean some other changes in the ceremony. But all things considered, wasn't that as far as the differences lay?' Reassured, he accepted, 'As you please, revered one.'

They walked homeward, the old man leading the way. Presently, they arrived at the mouth of the river. A little temple in crumbling stone stood by its banks. Close by was the priest's dwelling. It was a modest, quaint cottage, sparsely furnished. The simple, well-arranged exterior spoke to an elegance borne of simple living. All around could be discerned a caring hand, an eye for attention and detail.

Gesturing towards the temple, Vararuchi enquired of the idol of worship: was it Lord Vishnu? The old man nodded obsequiously, 'Yes, Sir. Is that your preferred school of worship too, wise one?'

Vararuchi dismissed the question pleasantly with a wave of the hand, 'Shiva or Vishnu, that is a matter of little consequence. Aren't they all but manifestations of the One?'

The irony of the remark was lost on the old man who sighed in relief. Vararuchi's response had lain to rest any misgivings he might have had about their differences. They were now in a neat little yard in the front of the cottage. Advancing to the doorway, the priest called out affectionately, 'Little one, are you there?'

The doorway parted but a little. At the sound of a tinkling of anklets, Vararuchi's eyes darted towards the door. But no form emerged from within. A demure voice sounded from behind the half-open doorway: 'Yes, what is it, Father?'

'A guest has come, little one. Bring him a seat so that he may be comfortable. Is everything set for the ritual, my dear?'

'All in place, Father,' the voice replied.

A hand appeared at the doorway, bearing an ornate wooden seat for the guest. The slender forearm presented an impressionable sight to Vararuchi's eyes. So too did a glimpse of petite feet covered in sensuous red patterns that glowed against the pallor of her skin. Laced caressingly around them were anklets of a pearly white.

Vararuchi's eyes darted involuntarily to the door once again as he heard the tinkle of anklets, languidly accompanying her movements as it reached his ears.

'We must thank our stars for this privilege of playing host to one as wise and revered as you,' the old man's remark interrupted Vararuchi's thoughts as he assumed his seat. The Vararuchi of old would have nodded matter-of-factly; neither flattered nor indifferent to the compliment. It was simply a truth beyond refute, as clear as the light of day. Why then did the oft-heard praise hurt him now; what was it that rankled within him? He tried to change the subject.

'Only the two of you that live here?' he asked.

'Yes, just my daughter and me. Today also marks the culmination of rituals of another kind.' Glancing at the door, he added in an undertone, 'the prospect of a perfect match for her.'

'Well,' he continued, 'you must be feeling hungry by now. We await your return after a holy dip in the river, Sir. All is ready here.'

Vararuchi grew impatient. He had to somehow break loose from these tedious, meaningless rituals. He had never intended to agree to the old priest's wish, after all. His mind was far away, thinking of an audience with Sage Shaaradwatam. Before him lay an arduous trek by day and night in the wilderness. But these poor things, he looked pityingly at the old man; he had not the heart to shun their little courtesies. He deliberated on his predicament at length. To leave them with no option than to themselves take back their invitation to him seemed the only way out. Avoiding the old man's eyes he gently reminded, 'Of the conditions I had mentioned… My presence hinges on their fulfilment.'

'Pray do express your wish, Sir, we are at your command,' the old man begged anxiously, 'as far as it be within our reach, they shall be fulfilled.'

Emboldened, Vararuchi spoke steadily, his voice dropping in an attempt at humility. His demeanour betrayed no wilful ill intent; though he might well have been addressing a foregone conclusion.

'Before I begin to eat, the gods and the demons are to be fed. The spread that you lay needs to be an eclectic one, with dishes and delicacies from this earth and the heavens. As a finale to the meal, I would like to consume three people. And after that, four are to bear my weight.'

The old man listened, aghast. At a loss to comprehend the request he stood. Was this the man supposed to be a scholar, an enlightened soul?

The sight of the trembling old man brought a smile to Vararuchi's lips. He could hardly hide his triumph at the priest's despair. Almost apologetic, he added self-deprecatingly, 'Please do not misunderstand my intent. It is all on account of a chance vow taken long ago.'

Presently, he rose. Both men well realized the futility of the moment. He had picked up his belongings and turned to depart, when a voice sounded from within the half-closed doorway. It had the effect of halting him mid-step.

'Father, please let our revered guest be, all his conditions shall be met,' the voice entreated. It might have been a humble plea to save the moment, but its assurance betrayed no doubt.

Vararuchi turned. There, arching by the doorway was the most beautiful woman he had ever seen. Ethereal, like the moon in its first flush, she stood, an alluring smile playing on her slightly parted lips. Her raven black hair hung low to her waist in flowing, wavy tresses. She possessed a graceful countenance, brimming with the vigour of youth. The sight of the maiden enchanted the young Vararuchi's austere gaze. With an effort he averted his eyes, looking at the old man instead.

The old man stood disbelieving, trying to understand how his daughter would fulfil this man's impossible conditions: But how are we to…'

The smile was now coy, distinctly playful. 'Please Father, all arrangements shall be made. Now if our guest would proceed to the river for the ritual dip…'

In a daze the priest repeated, shaking his head all the while, 'All arrangements shall be made Sir. If you could return after the holy dip...'

In silence Vararuchi turned towards the riverbank. As he strode past the little shrine, he was intrigued. Who was she, who showed the audacity to match her wits against his? Was her ethereal beauty matched by her intellect? His mind lingered on the enchanting form of the maiden. From within him there echoed a song, infinitely tender, touchingly true. It came not from the humming of the waters, nor the eerie quietude of the forest, not even from the birds as they called out in the morning air. On the wings of its lilt was awakened a feeling unknown to him until then. Once more he turned to the doorway where the beauty had appeared. It bore no trace of the maiden but he fancied he heard a merry tinkling of anklets from within.

'Vararuchi!' A voice he recognized as coming from his uneasy conscience called out to him, reprimanding. 'Are you an adolescent to be swayed so, by sensuous pleasures of the material world? An adult of a full thirty-five years, not for you the flippant imaginings of a flighty youth.' As though seeking refuge from the torment of his inner voice, Vararuchi quickened his steps to the river. Cradled in the glacial peaks of the Himalaya, the water was freezing cold in the wintry air. For a long time he lay in the water, unmoving; immersed in the numbing spell of its chill. Inwardly he was struggling in denial, fighting to resolve the arousal of a sensation all too new and forbidden. He prayed and hoped fervently that the sheer cold may quench the dark fire of his passion, that his being be soothed, mind and body by these icy waters. His lips moved silently:

*Frail of heart and spirit feeble,*
*Ill does it suit a man of mettle;*
*Mighty warrior it is unbecoming,*
*Banish the thought, arise unflinching.*

A resolute chant on his lips, Vararuchi lay languidly in the cold as the waters gently washed over him. It was a pacifying moment. When he rose from the dip his face had regained its colour, gone was the vulnerability of a while ago. Having regained his composure, he retraced his steps to the priest's dwelling. Outwardly he was once again the prodigious, austere scholar of renown.

The priest, who had been eagerly awaiting his return, welcomed him in. Leading him to their little room of worship he pointed, 'Within are figurines of the astral bodies—the nine planets of the Universe that stand for the legions of gods and demons and all the powers that be.' He begged of Vararuchi: 'The time is come for a propitiation, young Sir. Inside all is set for the rituals to begin. The ceremonial feeding of the gods and demons awaits you.'

Vararuchi stepped gingerly into the ritual chamber. So this was it, the first of his conditions that the gods and demons be fed. In silent deference to the old man's request, Vararuchi began with the rituals. It was an elaborate affair, with all the minutiae of a Vaishnavite ceremony. The ritual act of feeding accomplished, Vararuchi sat contemplatively. Eyes closed in meditation, he reaffirmed his faith in the pursuit of Truth. At length he emerged from the puja room. The old man invited him inside for lunch. He assumed his seat on an ornate wooden plank. The enchanting sight greeted his eyes again. The exquisitely delicate arm reappeared from within, bearing a dish outstretched towards the old man. One dish followed another in an arranged sequence as the old man lay the spread before Vararuchi on the earthen floor. As each dish changed hands from father to daughter, the old man would explain:

'This is plantain dipped in honey and ghee, in place of ambrosia, food of the gods.

'This makes for an offering to our forefathers who've ascended heavenward: curd with a sprinkling of ginger and pepper.

'And this is raw rice, steamed and piping hot—food for us mortals.'

As Vararuchi ate, the old man urged gently, 'You'll agree, Sir, the food is a sampling of many worlds.'

Again the tinkle of the anklets—taunting, enticing, matching his thinking measure for measure. Vararuchi finished eating and rose. No sooner had he washed his hands and passed into the antechamber that he glimpsed once again the maiden's hands. The outstretched arm now bore a tray of little vessels. 'What could it be now?' Vararuchi was intrigued.

'Betel leaves with lime to taste and a crackle of areca nut—the three people you would need to round off your meal, Sir.'

Hiding his chagrin, Vararuchi managed a reluctant smile. As he chewed on the leaves, the old man led him to an adjacent room. Inside, he explained: 'There, the foursome to support you as you rest.'

Inside was a four-legged wooden cot with a cotton mattress spread!

So this was it, he was truly outdone. 'I wouldn't have imagined!' he cried. 'Someone has outwitted me at last!' Vararuchi's thoughts escaped from his mouth.

'Not at all,' the old man hastened to add, thinking that perhaps his honoured guest felt slighted. 'Please do not take anything amiss. We have only tried to understand and follow your wishes.' Gesturing inside, he continued, 'It's all my dear Panchami's modest mind at work. Her diligence goes beyond matters of home and hospitality, you see. She has a keen interest in all aspects of knowledge. I can only hope it has brought you satisfaction.'

Vararuchi spoke truthfully, 'Her intelligence only reflects on your grace, holy one. Your scholarliness and intellect have passed in generous measure to your daughter. This poor traveller is the richer for having been your guest.'

The old man was overjoyed. 'We are fortunate to have served you. Please take rest; I'll be back after completing the rituals.' He retreated, leaving Vararuchi in the silence of the room.

The comfort of the cotton mattress in the cold room was inviting. A long while after the old man had left, Vararuchi lay awake, thinking. There was no tiredness, not even a suggestion of slumber as he lay, a trifle discomfited by everything that had transpired. He reflected on the change Sage Dhanvantari's hermitage had wrought on him. The new awakening stirred and lent beauty to all things in Nature. The realization he had there had affected him profoundly, beyond what words could express. He thought dimly: how did this spark take root? What was the unseen force that breathed life into his cold, calculating and analytical mind? Where did the music that wound its way into his thoughts, softening them with emotion come from? Vararuchi lay wondering.

Into the silence of the room crept a murmur from faraway. Softly, against the dreary silence of the afternoon, rose the sound of anklets tinkling. Shriller and shriller it grew, as though a presence had drawn closer. He felt he could reach out and touch the figure that now came gliding by his side, tantalizingly near. The swaying form, imagined rather than seen—a rustle of garment, anklets that danced in languid tandem to her steps—for poor Vararuchi, it was a moment of infinite seduction.

And then, just as gently as it had risen, the music ebbed, quieter and quieter it waned until all was silent again. Wasn't this a familiar strain, one he had heard at the meditation chamber of Sage Dhanvantari's hermitage? Vararuchi got up and paced the room. He was drawn to a little window by the wall that faced the bed. In the yard outside, he could see the stark outline of a banyan tree, its shadow stretched lazily in an afternoon siesta. In its comforting shade sat a girl, solitary and lonesome, a light veena resting in her arms. Exquisite, delicate fingers plucked at the string as she hummed a plaintive tune. His eyes were drawn to her feet as they rested gracefully, one against the other. The intricate rouge of the henna danced before his eyes, her anklets beckoned invitingly. For a long moment Vararuchi stood transfixed, unmoving. Something in him had melted. The years lay wasted behind him, a barren youth. An unbidden cry echoed from the wilderness of his conscience. It was a dirge, melancholic and pining—a fervent call for a mate, an anchor for his restless soul. For the first time ever, an unlikely expression had crept into the countenance of the ascetic: the pangs of longing.

The time neared for Vararuchi to set out once again in his quest. He presented himself to the old man.

'Wise one, you might well have heard of me. My name is Vararuchi, and I belong to a Brahmin family in a village not far from the capital. Seventeen years ago, when I was all of eighteen, I had attained the exalted seat of wisdom at the King's court. But,' Vararuchi shook his head dismissively, 'I never valued it much. I was restless, I sought to unravel a truth that was universal, a riddle that once unlocked would lay bare Nature and her secrets. It has been a long while since I set out on my search.' His voice grew heavy; his manner grave. The weariness of years suddenly sat heavy on his youthful countenance. 'Along the way I have gathered many a rebuke—cold, heartless, beastly they called me. But I wasn't one to mind. That truth could not but be coarse and bitter was my contention. To me it was unthinkable that it could be anything but so.'

'Of late though, it has been a season of awakening.' His face cleared as he attempted to explain. The words tumbled out in an unfamiliar vocabulary. 'I have begun to sense an innate emotion that suffuses everything with life, lends it a music of sweetness and grace. And now I have been led to the altar. It's been my privilege to see Beauty, Love and Intellect altogether as one—the very embodiment of Truth. For the first time ever I've been outwitted. In your daughter, I have found my perfect match; perhaps the only one who could understand me.'

The old man was overwhelmed. 'What do I say, the privilege is all ours…'

For Vararuchi it was the moment of truth, compelling and vulnerable. Words came to him naturally. 'The passions of the blood lash at my reasoning mind. I seek a bride, a deserving kin to my deed and conduct. With your consent, may I ask for your daughter's hand in marriage?'

The old man was speechless. A proposal from the renowned scholar Vararuchi; one who had attained the highest honour in the land! Anyway one looked at it, it was a godsend—the fruit of the day's fasting, or was it the propitiation for prosperous matrimony? And where did he stand—a poor ageing priest, eking out a living, counting his days to the grave? Panchami was admittedly bright and cultured, but what would become of her after his time? The more he dwelled on it, the more was he convinced this was the right match for her. He would, however, take his daughter's opinion.

She immediately acquiesced: 'Your wish is mine, dear Father,' she said.

Elated, the old man declared, 'Vararuchi! Your fame goes far and wide in our kingdom. I'm delighted to offer you my daughter's hand in marriage. There is, however, just one thing I must tell you. Panchami is my adopted daughter. She came into my life on a fateful night under the sign of Ashweena. It was the fifth day of the full moon, and I gave her the name Panchami. Ever since, she has been a doting child. The little that I know—the arts, sacred texts and the sciences—I have taught her. She shall forever be a dutiful wife to you.'

Vararuchi and Panchami were thus wed with due ceremony. The time drew near for a parting. Panchami bid farewell to her maid Dhaatri, who had always looked after her as her own child. By Dhaatri's side was her granddaughter Durga, Panchami's friend since childhood. Over the years their fondness and affection had taken on the nature of a familial relationship. Panchami now stood before her father, wordless, bowed with sorrow....The moment had come for the final parting. Father and daughter were overcome for words. Tears welled up in their eyes.

Vararuchi spoke comfortingly, 'For seventeen years I have been adrift in my wanderings. The trail has been treacherous and unforgiving. But now I feel I must return to the capital and settle down. The comforts of royalty and the luxuries of palatial living await me there. In peace and contentment, I shall pursue my learning.'

Turning to the blushing bride, Vararuchi spoke reassuringly, 'And lighter is my burden with Panchami by my side. She shall aid me in my quest, I'm sure.'

# What the Birds Foretold

The road to the capital led the newlyweds across many a village and town. The journey was tiring but it barely wore them out. The prospect of a new life together filled them with enthusiasm. Their hearts were full of hopes and aspirations for the years that lay ahead of them. Strangers to each other, detached from their moorings and brought together by fate, it was a momentous change for Vararuchi and Panchami. A troubled childhood and the rigours of ascetic living hadn't prepared Vararuchi for this change of scene. The concept of family life and the adjustments it called for was altogether new. For Panchami too, who had never had a family to call her own, it was an equally bewildering experience. Her foster mother, whose memory was a dull ache. A foster father—the man who had found her, raised her, and had been her only parent—and Dhaatri, who lived next door with her granddaughter Durga. Durga with whom she had grown up, laughed and cried, played and studied, the only friend she had ever known. Her life revolved around this little world of kinship without names, close knit and complete.

It had taken but a day, a ceremonial rite, for everything to change. Overnight, the playful girl had matured into a full-grown woman. A new world had chanced upon her unawares, a world that she had known to exist only in poems and plays so far. New sensations and experiences awaited her as she walked beside the man who was now her husband. No less was the bewilderment Vararuchi felt. In the eyes of the world he was a scholar, far removed from the ties that bound ordinary men. The nature of his calling had made him a grim, unrelenting man, who had grown old too soon. And to think that he now walked, like a young lover, beside a woman who was his wife! Their coming together had been set against an uninspiring background—the sleepy village by the banks of the Shipra River, a forgotten place where the comings and goings between people were few; hardly a place of much mingling. But this was of little consequence to the couple. The ascetic and his demure bride strode towards the capital. They might have been strangers, but as their feet fell in step and with hands clasped tenderly, all sense of unfamiliarity was gone. For many, many lives to come, they were one, woven inextricably by the thread of fate.

Night had begun to fall as they entered a forest. Twilight hung lightly over the woods, the ceaseless chatter of birds echoed in the air. Somewhere in the distance a bell rang, marking the hour of worship. In places, creepers had entwined and knotted in a sheltering web, roofed by leaves and flowers in bloom. Nature had set everything in motion for their first night together.

'We could rest here,' he murmured, observing the weariness in her face.

They sat under a tree by a brook that ran merrily among pebbles and stones. Its water sprayed white where it gushed against a stone in its path.

'Ah for a mouthful of water, and then a dip,' he observed, gazing at the stream.

She smiled endearingly at the suggestion. Framed by long black tresses and a graceful chin, her face shone with the radiance of the full moon on an inky black sky. Casting a sideways glance at him, she thought to herself: All her life she had known little of the world outside, sheltered in the cocoon of her own little world. And now...

'Is this me here, in this wilderness, at this hour, all alone with a young man I hardly know, a complete stranger? Strange, though, how his kindly charm sets my mind at rest, makes me forget all care. Where does this faith, this strength come from?'

She shook her head, at a loss to comprehend. The sight of the sheltering nest of creepers and vines was comforting. She crept inside and looked around. The ground felt soft beneath her feet. Thick grass made a mattress of green. Above, the branches and twigs tangled together, piecing together a view of the night sky. A gentle moonlight poured in. Looking at her taking in the moment, he lay outside, beneath the tree, head resting on his arms. She remarked, as though to herself, but loud enough for him to hear: 'It's beautiful...'

'For our first night?' he enquired softly, following her inside with his belongings.

The remark made her shy. She stood rooted, head lowered in embarrassment. He was sitting on the grass, looking at her keenly. He reached out and touched her. And then, ever so gently, his hands led her slender frame to rest on his lap. Her hair fell in wavy black tresses on the ground. His hands searched overhead and found a flower. Weaving it into her hair he spoke softly into her ear:

'For a love that's forever,
Though wilted now, this little flower.'

He lowered his face to hers; the intimacy of the moment was palpable. Now his breath was on hers, their lips close. All of a sudden she raised her hand, resisting. Her fingers pointed to something above, over his head.

'Look, we're being watched…two birds up there.'

She turned away, eyes closed in embarrassment. Vararuchi sat gazing at her unflinching. Holding her raised hands in his he pleaded gently, 'My dear, don't you see the beautiful stage that's been set for our coming together?' he gestured expansively, losing himself in description: 'The night sings a quiet song to the full moon. This dense forest stands bathed in its light. And amid this wilderness is our little home of fragrant flowers and leaves—cosy, sheltering and intimate. Come, sing me a song as you lie here in your lover's arms. A soothing caress to the coarseness of all these years I've been alone, the bitterness of experience, a fresh clean slate unto my soul. Come, sing to me of the very essence of nature, of life, of love.'

His eyes shone as he spoke and despite herself she was drawn to them, transported to an ethereal world. The reluctance of unfamiliarity faded, all sense of timidity was gone, she was now a woman transformed. Suddenly, she missed her home. The eerie nightscape around them faded and she was once again a little girl by her father's knee. It was the hour of worship at twilight as she wove flowers into a garland for the deity. The air was heady with the fragrance of camphor, the charred scent of stone lamps bathed in oil felt immediate. The glow of a thousand lamps from their little ledges illuminated the temple quadrangle. Sculpted steps led to a doorway that dazzled under the light from within. And as the bells pealed in obeisance they seemed to echo a refrain, 'No more of these for you, my little one, no more of charmed evenings by your father's knee.'

She realized with an ache that the coming of dawn and dusk held no expectation now, the landscape she had claimed her own seemed far, far away. Throwing her head wearily in his lap, she recollected: A house on a low hillock lush with fields of paddy. A thin rivulet that coursed by its edge. By the embankment stood an imposing tree. The rivulet ran full circle around the tree, coursing merrily as a thin stream before joining the Shipra River. At its mouth the river thundered into a cascade. The roaring of the waters rang in her ears. Carried away in its descent were leaves, twigs, and pieces of driftwood. Grimly, she reflected that hers too was a similar fate. Here today, gone tomorrow, she was like a castaway piece of driftwood at the mercy of the waves.

Her thoughts went back to the shrine at the riverbank. The swaying wind brought with it the fragrance of holy basil.

The temple premises were dotted with leaves and flowers in bloom. Overhanging boughs of an ashoka tree stood amid blossoms of dahlia and rhododendron. The air was aflutter with the chirping of birds. In the meadow, goats grazed contentedly. Tending to them were country girls, familiar faces to her. From their midst rose a song from a flute. It was her voice, she recognized. It was a familiar note, one he had heard at the prayer halls in Sage Dhanvantari's hermitage. Then again, it was the same murmur that had stolen into him as he lay resting at her home—that song of lost worlds, of hurt and of redemption. He sat listening, captivated, the words reached to him in a revelation. At length, when the song had ended, he exclaimed, 'It is you, Panchami, that I have been seeking in all my wanderings. In your eyes I see the glow of the celestial.'

Lovingly he embraced her, his fingers caressing her dense hair. Caressing her forehead he entreated, 'Where were you, my dear, all this time? And from where did you come, throwing light into the darkest recesses of my soul?'

The warmth of her lover's caress soothed her. She closed her eyes, his touch was tender, reassuring, and seemed to erase all her fears. A half-sleep came over her, she drifted languidly into it when all at once, a stabbing pain burned her between her eyes. It cut through her consciousness, knifing across her forehead. She recoiled from his touch, face contorted in agony as she pressed her hands to her forehead. His fingers had touched upon a raw nerve, an old wound had been awakened.

Shielding her face from his she entreated, 'Forgive me, it is an old wound; a mark of my birth that refuses to go away.'

'A birthmark? Why, where?' asked Vararuchi, concerned. Though he was taken aback by Panchami's reaction, he hardly expected the revelation that was to come.

'It's been seventeen years now, a curse I've carried as long as I can remember. A long time ago, as my father stood bathing by the banks of the Shipra River one late evening, he chanced upon a little raft made of plantain stems that the waves had washed ashore. In its hollow was a newborn girl child, mortally wounded and lifeless.'

She turned to face him, 'That wretched child, all of seven days and cast away to its end, was me.'

Vararuchi could not believe his ears. His mind grappled with the turn of events that had led to this. In his mind's eye he could see fate unfolding.

A pious Brahmin at his evening bath by the riverside. The sun had just set on the horizon, its afterglow lighting the atmosphere in a sombre light. The current was strong and washed ashore leaves and scattered twigs. Rocking in its wake was a small speck of light in the distance. Dancing with the waves, swerving unsteadily in its descent, the form drew closer and closer ashore. Little balls of fire flickering at its edges, the outline of a stoutly framed raft came into view. The Brahmin was intrigued; the raft was now within reach. Dimly he peered inside and recoiled in shock. Lying motionless was the body of a newborn child in a shallow pool of water collected at the bottom. A deadly thorn was nailed to its forehead. Blood oozing from the wound had knotted into a dark stain between the eyes. He held the child in both arms, easing it off the waters. He felt for traces of a heartbeat but there was none. Frantically, the old man rushed ashore. Could anything be done to save the little child? All he had was a native understanding of remedies and cures. Hurriedly, herbs and leaves were crushed to a paste and applied to the lifeless form. He coaxed its mouth open and dripped the extract from the herbs into it. But there was not a stir. Was there any hope at all? Time was running out; with a prayer on his lips he blew profusely into the ears and nostrils of the baby. He brought his mouth close to the lips of the baby and exhaled forcefully. There was a pause as the Brahmin took in his breath. All of a sudden, a cry came from the baby's lips. The old man was startled, then overjoyed. He hugged the child to his bosom. The evening light had now faded; the shrill cry of the child rang in the air.

The truth left Vararuchi numb. From over the din of his thoughts he heard her saying, '…was how I grew up. Father would always say that I was a blessed child. The mother I never knew had touched me with life, it was her kiss on my forehead that saved my life.'

'But,' she added wistfully, her hands touching her forehead, 'What a wound this that refuses to heal—like an unholy taint on the hour of my birth.'

So this was it. The girl that stood before him as his wife was the fateful child of yesterday. The years in between passed in a blur, the wailing rose in his ears again. The helpless cry of the newborn child grew louder and louder; in its nearness and feeling it had all the immediacy of the present. His face turned pale, his vision blurred. A foretelling had come true, the curse was fulfilled.

What was that, a hurried flapping of wings from above? In a trance Vararuchi looked up. In the moonlight, he could make out the silhouette of a pair of lovebirds. The male sang to his mate:

*See, my dear, in the shelter beneath*
*Sit a man and wife bound to each to each;*
*Seventeen years now, as destiny had writ,*
*The tale has unfolded true to script.*
*He, the fiery seeker of old,*
*That shunned kingly riches and gold;*
*Scholar, ascetic, sublime presence,*
*To whom knowledge was of the essence.*
*Yes, the very same that by writ*
*Had ordained that a life be sniffed;*
*Scholar, seeker, believer devout,*
*To remain celibate he had vowed;*
*Yet he has sought for a mate,*
*The one he had intended to forsake,*
*Yes, she a castaway in a wretched bed,*
*The seed of venom at her forehead,*
*And onward in the march of time,*
*A great progression in the line,*
*Not one, not two, but unto twelve,*
*Be the descendants they shall have,*
*A race unto each, an epic therein.*

His face flushed with fury at the song. He thought that he had nipped the threat in its bud. But the burden of fate hung heavily on his shoulders. Panchami sat cowering in a corner; the sudden change in her husband's demeanour had affected her profoundly....The peaceful setting of their coming together now seemed strangely ominous. He advanced to her threateningly and stood tall above where she sat; his eyes shone with anger.

'So it was you that I tried to escape,' he said, his voice cutting, 'The chosen one that awaited me, the fruit of my tribulations! How could this ever happen...' His voice trailed away.

'Oh no, oh no...that sought to be one with me—a soul mate,' his voice spat the word out.

She broke into tears, stung by the harshness of his words. Shrinking from him she mumbled, sobbing, 'Believe me, I beg of you; I know nothing of what you are talking about. All I know is that in my heart of hearts there's none but you. A life without you is unthinkable to me.'

He stopped, staring at her uncomprehendingly. In spite of himself he was touched by her plea. Her anguish was real, her helplessness palpable. He paused. Her form was visible in the light of a hazy moonbeam that coursed through the foliage. Outside, the moon stood in silent vigil to his outburst. The night landscape lay silhouetted; the darkness of the vegetation a shade over the night sky. Nothing had changed. He strained his ears to catch the hum of the night. Perhaps, he reasoned, his wrath was unfounded.

His countenance softened. It was still an effort to empathize but he began to try. The words came in a measured speech, treading precariously over his emotions.

'It is true, dear one, that our lives are intertwined inseparably. For each to live without the other is now unthinkable. You were meant to be mine; our communion has been foretold since the hour of your birth.'

With a sigh, Vararuchi continued, 'So much for the hand of destiny and its workings; together we shall surmount them all. If our lives have been nothing but a prophecy fulfilled, well then…' And at this his jaw hardened as he spoke through clenched teeth, '…it must equally be said that what is to come lies in our hands. That which I set to accomplish by myself is now the easier perhaps, with you by my side.'

What did he mean—'the hand of destiny, a prophecy fulfilled…?' Panchami sat silently, looking timidly at her husband. The note of consolation that had crept into his voice frightened her, the rhetoric of his words puzzled her even more. Why did he mention the hour of her birth? What did he intend for them to 'accomplish together'? Her eyes followed him as he turned and spoke threateningly, as though to someone up above:

'Listen, oh powers that be, you unseen forces that shape destiny. Let it be known that Vararuchi has accepted your challenge. This is no weakling's word. I speak with the assurance of one that has mastered the sciences. Your words make tall claims—twelve descendants to come, a lineage unto each…those are grand words.'

He turned slightly, gesturing to Panchami, 'Your divine intervention had once saved a life, fulfilling a prophecy in its wake. In the light of all that's passed, would you do the same with her children too? We shall see. The path ahead holds no perils for me.'

Reassured with the proclamation, he turned to Panchami. She wilted from his gaze, shrinking into a corner. The sight discomfited him. He was torn by the irony of the circumstance. In a moment of weakness, he had deluded himself into the relationship. And in a cunning sleight of hand, destiny had gained on him.

He held her close and spoke gently. His voice dropped to a whisper but there was no mistaking the resolve in his words. 'To live happily ever after with you, in the royal comfort of the capital, pursuing knowledge in peace and contentment to the end of our days—that would've been my fondest desire. But now it all seems impossible. For our life ahead is a wearisome journey. Unmoored and restless we shall tread on its treacherous path to wisdom and understanding. What has happened so far is only a foreshadowing. But Vararuchi is not one to be swayed by his destiny. He shall be known through time as the one that dared…', his voice rose, pronouncing each word emphatically, '…that lit the torch that showed the way.'

Perturbed by her silence, he asked, 'Well Panchami, are you here with me?'

She remained mute. Perhaps the full impact of his words hadn't quite sunk in. Or was it the opposite—that she had fully understood his intentions, and was shocked, speechless? But then, Panchami was not a mere village girl naïve and foolish. Her grasp of affairs went beyond the obvious. In a world of uncertainties, her intuition had been honed to perfection. Which way to follow, which ones to sidestep—her judgement was astute, informed. And therefore, she betrayed neither alarm nor agreement at his words. All she would suggest was a saner recourse, a humane approach that steered clear of all extremes. She pondered over the nature of his quest, his rebellion against fate, life itself. She found something strangely amiss. What place had love and compassion in such a quest, she wondered. And what of kinship, of family ties…It seemed inconceivable to her that a seeking could be so cold, so devoid of heart. Carefully, she chose her words:

'In your enlightened view, the element of love…'

'Panchami!'

Her gentle overture was rudely cut short. Vararuchi would hold back no more. His look and gesture forbade further discussion. His voice had the ring of authority: 'Arrogant scholar, rude man of learning, conceited intellectual—these are epithets I have, perhaps deservedly, gathered along the way. But let none doubt the expanse of my knowledge.'

Half asking, half decided, he continued, 'Come with me if you are willing to stand by my side in this journey. Our ordeal by fire has begun.' He was seized with the gravity of the moment. 'No ordinary beginning is this; it marks the first step in man's might against destiny.'

Needless to say, his was the last word, leaving no room for counter or for query. Concealing her dismay she went to his side, head bowed in deference. 'There will be no other path for me but for the one that's lit by you,' she murmured.

Her submissiveness pleased him; her faith in him was comforting. Now reassured, his hands gently played with her hair, his fingers stroking her forehead. All of a sudden, he jerked away as though reminded of something. Drawing her hands together he tenderly kissed them, touching them to her forehead. 'It is just the first day since you left home into a whole new life. The change of scene is sure to have worn you out. What you need is a good night's rest. Who knows, it could well be elusive in our journey together.'

# The Abandoned and the Orphaned

Spring was in the air, and in the minds of the young lovers, showering its bounty in a splash of colour and fragrance. The sweet scented darling buds that bowed to the playful wind, the wind that carried the music of birds chirping gaily—it was a delirious orchestration of nature's sounds and smells. In their newfound companionship, Vararuchi and Panchami immersed themselves in each other, enjoying the season of celebration in full measure. They crossed mountains, valleys, and towns. As the ground beneath their feet gave way to harsher terrain, they made light of distances on horseback and camel. The waters of the Holy Ganga, the Krishna, and the mighty Godavari fell behind them with barely a ripple as they continued further south. Presently they neared the outskirts of a town. They had been travelling for a long time. For Panchami, the days and nights of intimacy had cemented the bittersweet revelation of a new life together. Pointing to a shade by the wayside she said, 'Look, shall we rest a few days here… something inside me is stirring. I can neither stand nor walk…'

He turned to her, she looked weak and exhausted. Her legs gave way and she clung to him. He supported her frail body and carried her to the shade by the wayside. Gently, he seated her by the tree and rested her head on his lap. He looked searchingly at her, concerned. As her gaze met his, the unease flitted. She turned red, her cheeks flushed with embarrassment. In an instant, Vararuchi understood. His face shone in a rapture that came from he knew not where.

'The beating of a new life, my sweetheart? Ah, the flowering season has borne fruit, it is Nature at work.'

She smiled in agreement and asked again, 'Shall we rest here for a few days...' Looking down at her stomach she continued, 'Can't we wait until this...'

He thought for a moment and then said, 'No, you are not to be idle at this time. When the hour comes I shall tell you. Vararuchi has studied the science of birth too.'

They rested by the shade of the tree, reviving themselves before setting out again. The days and nights were thorns in their quest but they trod on them unflinchingly. The heat, the cold, and the rain they bore relentlessly in their pursuit. In her hour of need, Vararuchi was care personified. He nourished her with fruits and fresh water. With his knowledge of Ayurveda he made her a mixture of herb extracts. His soothing caresses on the back and limbs brought her relief from aches. As she slept he stood guard over her. She was to him a trembling flame to be shielded from the elements, a tender blossom that might wither in the passing breeze. As for Panchami, she was beginning to discover the intensity of his passion. His stoic devotion to her well-being was overwhelming, placing her at the mercy of his affections. But she grew to accept it as a necessity, a natural equation in their relationship. And with it came the realization that a bondage of love was perhaps no bondage, but real freedom.

Many days later, on a summer afternoon, Vararuchi and Panchami found themselves the only travellers in a vast stretch of a farmland. Sheltering creepers and flowering trees hung over the lush valley. With the swaying wind, boughs heavy with fruit shook and ripened fruits fell from their branches. A breeze came descending from the heights. It had cast a spell in the air, in its wake the day hung light and languid over the valley. From a cleft in an opening from high, the sun glinted on the waters of a brook. On a mat of green, Panchami lay resting, exhausted, leaning her weight on her husband's supportive frame. Raising herself with an effort she whispered meekly into his ear, 'I can't bear it anymore… this pain inside…'

He nodded in understanding. Intuitively, he had divined of the coming. The throes of creation, a necessary rite of passage for all living beings. Comfortingly, he said, 'It is the pain of creation, no escaping it. We can do nothing but to face it with courage.'

She was silent, too weak to reply. A wave of pain coursed through her, leaving her giddy, nauseated. He continued, 'It is the pain that marks creation for its own, remember.' Gently, he raised her and took her to an alcove by the side. Inside, intertwining branches and twigs made for a cosy shelter from the elements. Setting her to rest in a corner he rose; the arrival was impending. Turning to her as he took leave he said, 'Have no worry, I shall wait outside.'

He stood in the shade of a tree, leaning on its trunk, waiting for the moment. It was a tense interim that brought with it a creeping sense of unease; anxiety and guilt began to wrack at his conscience. To think that he had brought her here in this wilderness, all alone to fend for herself this unbearable ache at a time when she needed the care and attention of a woman the most… Almost without his knowing there came unbidden the thought of his mother. And he found himself rueing her absence at this momentous hour. What divinity, what sense of occasion her presence would have lent, he lamented. In spite of himself, the thought of the impending arrival made him nervous. There rose in his veins a trembling that made his hair stand on end. It was undeniable, this primal instinct for perpetuation that coursed through him in a wave of ecstasy. The realization dawned on him tellingly.

'Vararuchi! A glorious fatherhood awaits you! In the saga that passes unabated generation to generation, here's a thread all your own. In the hand that clasps your own the baton is passed; a whole chapter begins anew. New paths to tread, new learnings, new attainments in an ever-widening horizon…by this, your next in blood.'

He was jolted from his reverie by a hurried noise from above. He looked up, his gaze following a familiar flapping of wings from high above. Sure enough, like an evil come revisiting, perched on the branches were the lovebirds. As

Vararuchi looked on, dazed, the male spoke to his mate in a voice of disdain:

*Remember the pundit of yore*
*The rebellion against fate he bore*
*The fool that sought to write anew*
*The writ of fate, the truth we knew*
*That set adrift a poor newborn*
*At its forehead a venomous thorn*
*Only to reclaim her many years hence*
*All his vows an elaborate pretence*
*And with her here in the wilderness*
*The moment of truth, of tenderness*
*His wait is anxious, all apprehensive*
*For inside stirs the fruit of his missive.*

Vararuchi sat listening astounded. The words stung him into silence. He felt a burning between his eyes, the heat of something sharp that set his teeth on edge. The malicious, mocking allusion of the prophesying birds had found its mark, the humiliation was more than he could bear. He struggled to contain himself. At length, when a measure of composure had returned, he was beset by guilt. The birds had a message he could not dismiss. Wasn't he indeed in an unmindful wait? What of his loud-mouthed proclamations and taunts against the workings of destiny? Indeed, the object of his waiting spoke more eloquently than words; wasn't it symbolic of a failed endeavour? His mind went to the languorous moments of their first night. It was to have been a glorious beginning, but no, with it had come the bitter reminder of a past folly. He well remembered the indignation of the moment, the retort of a man who had first tasted defeat. What had come of his lofty pronouncements then? And how was he to justify his present circumstance?

Inwardly he resolved, but this time there was a mellowing. 'The truth of the matter is accepted, it was an unwitting moment that did me in. But listen, you powers that be, the rest is yet to unfold, as you shall see.'

His mind worked away in anger at the birds and their inopportune appearances. They would have come to gloat over this second misstep and rejoiced on seeing Vararuchi plumb the depths yet again, he reproached himself. What has come of your scholarly defences, your verses in vicissitude? Has the lust for flesh dimmed your sense of purpose? To think that the sensuous delights of a lowly bred girl had weakened the steely resolve of Vararuchi. Why then this tortuous pretence of sacrifice? Life had beckoned him in all its guises, each with a wealth of promise—in the lap of luxury in the capital amid kingly grandeur, the sanctimonious living of a pious Brahmin in the countryside, or the cosy comforts of a home, a family, a life of marital bliss. Was this then a fate befitting the Vararuchi that had held claim to the exalted seat of wisdom? The Vararuchi who had held that man's destiny was a measure of his strength of will, that one's end lay within oneself? The drive that led him till here—was it failing him now? Should a lifetime of penance be forsaken in a momentary human bondage? Inside of him there sounded a cry of awakening:

*Frail of heart and spirit feeble*
*Ill does it suit a man of mettle.*

The words sounded ominous, echoing from his yesterdays, falling as though shed from the age-old branches of time. He trembled, bristling at the memory the lines had brought. With an effort, he shook himself free and rose determinedly. Fixing his gaze at the branch from where he had heard the singing, he let forth: 'Listen, you gods of destiny, our scores are not settled yet, you haven't even begun to comprehend the prowess of Vararuchi.'

The challenge hung in the air even as the words rang out with the incisiveness of a slingshot. He paced up and down, struggling to contain himself. The trace of defeat was undeniably there, and yet, he could not bring himself to face it. He muttered under his breath to himself, or was it to catch the ear of Panchami who lay writhing in the alcove?

'In an unhinged moment of forgetting, I had remarked that time may well follow its course for all I care. But no, the reality of my experience repeatedly tells me otherwise. Caught in the intimacy of the moment, I was simply following a primal instinct. Surely Time is not to be taken as lightly as that. It is to be tamed, harnessed, and led along the path of one's will.' A lump rose in his throat, 'Else, there remains no hope for man.' His face settled grimly as he decided. 'Harsh though it may be on you Panchami, I have but no other recourse. Forgive me, for this is my chosen path.'

As though on cue there rose from inside the shelter an endearing cry. A newborn had sounded its coming into the world! Vararuchi paused to listen. An expression of pure delight stole through his features, softening them in the late evening light. He went to enter, feet poised at the threshold. A moment's indecision—that was all; he reined in his thoughts. Resolutely, his foot retraced its step. From faraway inside he heard Panchami calling out, 'Look, a son has been born to us. Come in, bless him, my revered. For his rites of passage into our world...'

But he would pretend to have not heard her. Turning his back to the shelter where she lay with child, Vararuchi hurriedly stepped back into the woods. But there was no escaping the cry. It followed him wherever he went, shrill and piercing, a pointed quill that tore at his consciousness. It resounded eerily in the thicket, a malevolent harkening to an episode almost buried in his memory. In nearness and poignancy it blended strangely with a cry from long ago. He paused, listening intently despite the urge to flee his memories. This cry, where had he heard this before? The mist cleared and the echo sounded a note of the familiar. Memory was never as welcome as it was at the moment, and he was once again at a ruined shrine by the riverbank, witness to the celebration of a birth long gone by: a hutment of poor peasants, an ancient banyan tree in a shrine of crumbling stone, a river at its mouth, the Shipra riverbank. The past cast its shadow into the present as he stood listening. No, the cry he now heard had a rather unlikely note of reproach, a sting of malice, an edge that he could not miss. Why did this sound familiar? All of a sudden, the near-forgotten episode surfaced.

A small rectangular raft fashioned out of white plantain stumps—the very sacrificial vehicle for carrying the blood-red remains in serpent worship. At the four corners were pegged flaming torches soaked in oil, shining light into the floor of the raft. In its shallow bed lay a newborn child, an unwitting victim of its hour of birth and what it foretold. Gently, they lowered her to rest on the cold mat of the floor. The child twitched its tiny arms and legs playfully as though tickled by the touch. But this was a harmless prologue to the deadly play that was to follow. Its soft flesh came under the venomous thorn and the child squealed at the uncomfortable pressure. It felt uneasy, it felt like pain. And as the thorn was struck in its first numbing impact into the tender flesh, the child screamed in terror. But to no avail. The act was ordained, the intentions were the best. A kingdom's salvation depended on it; a child born under the evil eye was a threat to the state and its people. Bit by bit, the thorn pounded into the child's forehead even as the late evening air was rent with its helpless cries. The act was carried out by another Brahmin of the royal court. He had presided over the affair in the manner of a master of ceremonies so that things were as they ought to be, that there be no hitch in proceedings, that there be no straying from the rulebook. He prompted another by his side in the recital of hymns, hymns that would free the kingdom from the child's malevolent legacy. But already the wails of the child were drowning out all chanting, distracting all ritual. He chanted louder and louder. His own voice sounded distant, unrecognizable, subdued in the rising din. As the waters swept the rudderless boat in a dizzying downswing, there resounded in the air an unending refrain. Above the hum of the waves it persisted, a haunting omen of revenge, of hate, of betrayal. In his earlier years of guilt the memory had been a tortuous reminder. He had imagined the omen in the form of a black serpent entwining around his conscience, fastening at the neck as he gasped for breath. He dared not look back at it. The vision had haunted him for an eternity. And to think that now the curse had come revisiting.

'Panchami, oh dear…I can't, I can't…' he murmured, faint with exhaustion. On his countenance was the fatigue of exertion. 'Leave me alone, free me, away with it all, it never happened, it never really…the sacrifice, the ritual by the riverbank…' His agonized mind saw the poor grief-stricken parents. They stood watching, mute witnesses to a fate they didn't choose. Like ghosts seeking redemption, the apparition hung in his mind, an accusing finger pointing to his conscience.

'No, no leave me alone… Free me from this snake around my neck that could hiss and snap at any moment. Am I to suffer this avenging, is it a settling of scores this that destiny seeks?' Anguished he called out to her, 'You may come with me Panchami, this ordeal is more than I can bear alone.'

Agitated and disturbed beyond measure, he continued pacing up and down until, at last, he rested against a bed of rocks. He drew a deep breath and closed his eyes. But peace of mind was not to be his. A familiar visage swam before his eyes. In a daze he recognized it as that of his long-lost brother. But where was this—an ethereal netherworld of blood and gore! A resting place of the dead, an open-air theatre of the occult—there stood his brother brandishing an axe amid a circle of fiendish looking men. Behind him loomed a darkened temple, its tower silhouetted grimly against the evening sky. Still in a daze, Vararuchi identified it as the shrine of Raktha Chamundi, situated by the Kali ghats. The infamous altar where men were sacrificed to propitiate the deity! In his vision his brother stood on its hallowed floor, ready for the ghastly ritual. The blood of centuries had stained the floor many a shade darker than its natural black. A pillar facing the floor was at the centre of a spectacle about to unfold. There, hands tied at the back and feet fastened to the pillar by ropes stood the limp form of a man. He wore a robe of blood-red, and on his neck was strung a chain of red beads. With bloodshot eyes, he watched in terror as the ritual began. The blade of the axe glinted eerily in the twilight as his brother advanced towards the victim. The guards encircling him chanted verses in unison, their rhythm ascending as he neared the pillar. The crowd roared as one in anticipation, the prisoner looked forlorn and helpless at the executioner. But his sense of desolation was lost on the spectators. To them, enthusiastic do-gooders of the state, the killing was an act of cleansing, a supreme sacrifice that held the promise of good times to come. Prosperity of the land and freedom from sin and suffering were now within their reach thanks to this act of appeasement to the Goddess.

Louder and louder rose the chant as his brother neared the victim, his axe poised to strike. Now the chanting had reached a feverish pitch, a sing-song of riotous cacophony. The demoniac guards broke into a dance, flailing their arms and legs as they shuffled in a whirl around the prisoner. Their movements became frenzied, a deafening roar rose until it all looked like a pack of fiends gone mad. The din continued, faster and faster until the climactic moment. The hangman's axe rose and swung mercilessly. The body of the sinner was split in two, the crowd erupted in ecstasy. His brother withdrew his axe, it was bathed in blood. The sight sickened Vararuchi; he shrank visibly in fear and loathing. He shouted out loud, 'How did you, my loving brother of old, chance upon the company of fiends such as this? That you would come to believe in this archaic practice! Can wellness and prosperity be bought at the cost of a life? Can such a nihilistic ritual promise deliverance from ill omen and suffering?'

Caught in the frenzied ritual, his brother turned to Vararuchi. In look and manner he was the picture of the devil. He swore incorrigibly and shouted, raising a finger at Vararuchi. Vararuchi strained his ear but could not catch what his brother was saying in the din. The long years of separation had denied them the familiarity of a shared tongue even. The nuances of a language they once shared were now forgotten.

But the import of his words was tellingly clear; the raised finger signalled a reproach. And Vararuchi read a meaning that was as undisguised as it was cutting.

'But you too, Vararuchi!' the raised finger seemed to say. 'To be sure, you are no more the poor innocent brother I knew. And is what I do any different from what you do, really? At its heart aren't our motives the same? You, cultivated and calculating, cloaked in the gentility of faith, while here I stand with not a hint of pretence, primitive and stark. Yet, what we practise is the same: murder in the name of sacrifice, by way of ritual.'

He was awakened from his dream by the child's cry and a worried Panchami calling out to him. With a start, he returned to the present. As he looked towards the shelter where the mother and child lay, his mind was made up. Nothing now to ponder or even consider. His was now to set out on the path he had chosen, a path that would follow the leading of his own will.

Resignedly, he took care of every need of Panchami's, unasked. He brought rich foods from the wild for her to eat. He administered healing herbs and cooked for her a nutritious mix of pulses, grains, and milk. All these he arranged from outside the shelter without ever stepping inside. An extended hand inside was all he would venture into her presence. Her enquiries from inside were met with brief, monosyllabic responses or sometimes a nod.

So dutiful yet dispassionate, but why is he so, wondered Panchami. It puzzled her, brought her disquiet to see her child's father in such detachment. She remembered their first night together, the nuptial bed of green, the moonlight seeping through the vines overhead—and the revelation of her birthmark. Then as now, something seemed to have taken possession of him, he had become a man disturbed. All her pleas to come see the child and take it in his arms fell on deaf ears. Morose and grim, Vararuchi remained on the fringes, ever attentive yet unyielding. Familiar now with his ways, Panchami too refrained from any provocation. Thus they lived on either side of a wall of silence and resignation. She would tend to the child by herself, rocking his tiny frame on her shoulder as she gently lulled him to sleep.

To Vararuchi, who lay under the canopy of a starry, soulless sky distanced from the sights and smells of human bondage, the lullaby sounded like a torment. The hushed refrain washed over him, weakening him as he tossed about, tortured. In his mind it evoked, with tragic precision, all the misery of the human condition and its attendant grief. Unceasing, the mother's song echoed in the forest, solitary and forlorn, washing over him in waves of reproach. At length when he could not bear it anymore, the obscurity of the wilderness was a welcome refuge. He fled into its depths, out of earshot, out of mind.

Many days passed as Panchami and Vararuchi continued their separate lives. Eventually, however, Panchami was unable to contain her curiosity. Standing at the threshold of their little home she looked out. A detached Vararuchi lay under the shade of a tree nearby. Inside, the child had begun to cry. Vararuchi awoke with a start. Head bowed, Panchami stood before him. Her face was suffused with a newfound radiance. Disarmingly, she entreated of him, 'Our child is now all of ten days old. For once could you step inside and see him, I beg of you.'

His face averted, Vararuchi replied, 'No, I do not wish to.'

Panchami eyed him searchingly. 'Do not wish to…?' Her voice trailed away, faltering in disbelief.

But he was not one to relent. Decisively, he declined. 'It is not for Vararuchi to be bound by ties of affection. True, he has had to accept matrimony, but not for him a familial life. No, no, I do not wish to see.'

Half turning to the child she persisted, coy and demure. 'He is the very image of his father. Come take him in your arms. Kiss him once, I beg you.'

Vararuchi gathered his staff and belongings. There was a faraway look in his eyes, and when he spoke there was not a touch of feeling. 'May I remind you, Panchami, that ours is an ascetic way of life? Creation has its rightful place in it. But care, nurture, and upbringing—these are worldly affectations and therefore not suitable for us.'

Unable to understand, she asked, 'Not for us? For whom, then?'

Came the detached reply: 'No other than this bountiful Nature. It is She that has welcomed this flowering.'

A wail escaped Panchami, 'Oh God…'

He grew impatient. 'Your God may save you. Let the child be, it's time for us to leave.'

Her worst fears were confirmed. 'For us to leave? And what of the child…to leave him here?' she asked, half-doubting, half-pleading.

Again she was met with indifference. 'Yes,' replied Vararuchi, his voice rising. 'Very much so. Are you going back on your word now? At the beginning of this journey I had made my intentions clear. Ours is a journey without end. We are wayfarers in the labyrinth of Time, in search of the ultimate Truth. In our quest we have to live outside worldly trifles. Have you well forgotten the terms of our endearment?'

She was beside herself with tears. Between muffled sobs she managed to speak. 'But he's all of an infant. Who is to take care, feed…'

His reply was sharp and bewildering. 'The child's mouth—has it formed?'

Panchami was perplexed. Half-indignantly she asked, 'But can you not hear it cry? Would a child cry without a mouth?'

'In that case, we should be proceeding. Such a child shall surely find its feed. And perhaps,' he continued in a voice heavy with sarcasm and irony, 'it too shall find a saviour. Come, let us go.'

The hint was not lost on her. But this was scarcely the time. She had not lost all hope yet. Clinging desperately to the last shred of hope she begged, 'Never ever shall I ask anything more of you. Just this once…please…you need not bother at all, I'll look after him all by myself. Please, just this once.'

'Panchami,' Vararuchi thundered with finality. 'This is a vow that brooks no going back. You may remain here if you find it right. But for me, I have to pursue my path.'

He gathered himself with an effort and set afoot. He was thankful for the gathering darkness that hid his face, for it mirrored all the conflict in his being. Thankful too that none could hear the voices that raged within him. The right and the wrong lay divided along an indistinct line of grey as he strove to justify his actions. All his primal instincts railed against him. He had left behind a wife and a child, all alone in the wilderness. Up ahead, the future was an enigma, a question mark he had resolved to fathom. Torn between the two he trod on, unsure and filled with self-doubt, and yet, unwilling to look back.

For a long while, Panchami stood sullen and unmoving, gaping at her husband's retreating figure. It was the moment of reckoning and she was perplexed and torn with grief at her strange predicament. Nothing in her upbringing had ever prepared her for this. She had no clue of her options in a situation such as this. In a fit of helplessness she called to her foster father, the living God she knew: 'O Father, give me strength.'

Would the father have heard his daughter's impassioned plea? The father who had appeared fortuitously—no, divinely—as the hand of Providence that saved a poor child from her watery grave? Who, having given away his doting child in marriage, now sought peace and salvation in his twilight years. The old man that trudged a weary trail in the mountainous passes of Badrinath and Kedarnath—would he ever hear the echo from far away? Was it a heavenly messenger that bore the cry? The utterance appeared to have exerted a charm. She fell silent. Perhaps it was her father's large-heartedness that reassured her at the hour of calamity. As has happened to you, your child too shall endure, was the unspoken refrain. Or perhaps it was bravado occasioned by the sheer desolation of the moment. Whatever it be, it wrought a miraculous change in Panchami's demeanour. She was now a woman pacified, her choice was made. In a voice crumbling with emotion she whispered, 'Our fate is to remain faithful, devoted wives unwavering in the service of our husbands.' Wistfully looking heavenward, she continued, 'But are we to be denied even motherhood ? A terrible predicament indeed for a woman…my God!' Her cry would not have reached Vararuchi, who had all but vanished into the distance.

Preparing to leave, Panchami looked inside the little shelter that had been home to their little one. The child bristled for attention, crying. She laid him gently on a mattress of flowers. Bending low over his diminutive form, she kissed him on the forehead. 'My little darling, your mother had suffered a similar fate: a venomous thorn here. Alas, my poor baby.'

The mother's grieving kiss appeared to work magic. The child cried no more and instead, silently looked into his mother's eyes. She took him in her arms, holding him tightly to her for the last time, never wanting to let go of what was so much a part of herself. She kissed him again and again, dreading the moment that was inevitable. At last, she lay him down with a prayer.

'My little darling bundle of joy! Forgive me for what I have to do. A heartfelt kiss is all this mother has to give you. It is the very same that my mother had blessed me with, years ago. May you grow to live long, become a scholar, a man of learning and great compassion. In the fire of your sacrifices as Agnihotri, the Lord's chosen one, wash away this—the sin of a helpless mother.'

The child lay unblinking, as though comprehending his mother's last words. Her heart heavy, she kissed him tenderly once more. It was to be the last moment of indulgence. Rising from the placid form of the child she turned and fled. Far in the distance was a blur that was Vararuchi. She followed him doggedly, never turning back, not once looking over her shoulder. But the night was not without vigil. Overhead, from the branches on high, the air was rent with birds singing.

# A Folly Repeated

The choice between a dutiful wife and a nurturing mother was a decisive one. If she were to recall the episode that changed her, the remorse would have been shattering, all consuming. But Panchami was never one to be overcome. Disconsolate but resolute, without as much as a backward glance, the incident was buried. Her reconciliation with the man she followed in all his vanity was complete. In its wake she forsook the little, natural joys that life afforded. Any thought of fulfilment for oneself simply did not exist. His wearying pursuits led them from town to hinterland, from one school of learning to the next. From the observatory of Bhaskaracharya, to Sankaranarayanabhattapadar's centre for studies in mathematics, or scholarly discourses on Kautilya's *Arthashastra*—all were grist to the mill in Vararuchi's relentless strides into the expanse of knowledge. By his side forever, she feigned an interest and appreciation she had never possessed. Her only moments of happiness were the rare sessions on classical theatre and poetry. Her intuitive intelligence was awakened and she was drawn naturally to literature. But here too, what distressed her was her husband's preoccupation with analysis and grammar, ignoring the elements of abstraction and beauty. Theirs was a complete coming together of opposites, both in temperament and taste. The scholar and his reluctant companion presented an unlikely picture of a happy married couple. But here again, it was perhaps the hand of destiny that led them unknowingly in their travails. It guided Panchami in ways subtle yet strong. It instilled in her an enviable perseverance and understanding. And thus, they survived in a sustainable arrangement of the gods, saved from an otherwise certain faltering.

Twenty years passed by thus, an arduous stretch of time filled with harshness and bitter experiences. Around them, Nature beckoned in all its colourful gaiety. As one season gave way to another, it brought with it a variety and beauty of its own. The good earth was awash with riotous hues of a silken carpet, changing colours as it glinted in the sunlight. Ever an alluring host, it signalled a welcome to partake in the season of rejoicing and merriment. In the tender sapling that grew to a tree, the flower that bloomed on its branch, the fruit that followed its shedding, and within the fruit the seed that held the tree of the morrow—the natural order of life continued unabated.

Vararuchi was unabated in his quest. Single-mindedly he persisted, caught up in the fervour of his investigation. Nature and all her charms were lost on the austere ascetic. Amid the aridness of their living, there shone nevertheless a glimmer of springtime. Devoid of any comfort and luxury, like a cactus in full bloom, Panchami blossomed; motherhood came calling, not once but many times over. She conceived ten more children. And history repeated itself every time. All were abandoned by the wayside in the course of their journey. Solitary and trusting, with a faith as strong as it was naïve, she let go of them one after the other. Motherhood was her greatest ordeal and agony.

Looking back, the passage from her early days of innocence to the present state of mind was momentous, a change that she could scarcely believe. The little girl who grew up by the banks of the Shipra River belonged to another time and age. She knew no needs or desires; sorrow was unknown. She had found care and affection in the close-knit circle of three people, who were her natural family: the priest who had saved her from death had been her guardian and caretaker. In his shade the early loss was never felt, he was the living father she knew. There was Dhaatri, the old lady that helped in services at the temple. In her presence she experienced the love of a mother. Then there was Dhaatri's granddaughter Durga, her soulmate. Durga with whom she would laugh and cry, share all her experiences growing up. In that glorious childhood of sunshine and laughter, they drew from all that life had to offer two wide-eyed, innocent children. Always together at the village school for study and in prayer at twilight hour at the temple—these were her fond memories of childhood. Indeed, every episode in memory seemed incomplete without Durga. Together they frolicked in the river, chased butterflies, and followed the cry of parrots in their bamboo grove. The swing by the rasala tree in the temple yard was an object of their endless amusement. Back then in the formative years of their growing up, she had always been a delicate child, quick to break into tears. Durga would chide her brittleness; 'touch-me-not', she would call her.

Touch-me-not indeed!

Would Durga believe her eyes if she were to see the transformation that time had wrought on her childhood friend?

She threw her mind back to the fortuitous occasion in the month of Karthika many years ago. It was the ninth day of the full moon marked by customary rituals and fasting. The handsome Brahmin youth had come as an opportune guest and left with her hand in his. The turn of events had taken her by surprise. The moment of parting lay vivid in her memory. Her heart was numb with sadness. Ahead lay the promise of a happy married life with the young man who had been a stranger till then. How foolish she had been at the time! He was a good deal older than her, eighteen years her senior and a man of great learning. He had already gained renown as the steadfast seeker who had declined the exalted seat of wisdom at the King's court in order to pursue knowledge. The timing of his visit had seemed almost preordained. She had had her doubts then. When father revealed to her that the young man sought her hand in marriage, she had been taken aback. She was not yet ready, marriage and family life were vague concepts at her tender age. She found no space to relate her notions and concepts to the young man that sat waiting. All of a sudden the descent to reality had taken her by surprise. Somehow, it seemed all too swift and short to make up her mind. To be honest, knowing the man and his formidable reputation, she could never have refused. She had stood, head bowed and tongue-tied. Her father had mistaken it for reluctance. Consolingly he added, 'If you are not in favour then that's all right too, child. The young man has simply expressed a wish. We can voice our opinion too, can't we?'

Durga interjected, reading her mind, 'She never said so, Uncle, did she? It's because she dreads the thought of leaving us and going away, isn't it Panchami?'

Father continued understandingly, he could feel for her at this time of indecision.

'Well, marriage is inevitable, my child. As for me, my time is limited. How many years have I left? With your future entrusted in safe hands, I can take leave of the world. It is my great desire to find salvation in the foothills of the Himalaya. I shall retreat to the end of my days in the mountains of Badrinath or Kedarnath.' He paused, 'This appeared a promising prospect and it is time for you as well, Panchami, which is why I asked. If you're not happy I'll say so willingly.'

But Durga had been ecstatic. 'Didn't you hear that, Panchami? A promising prospect, such a nice proposal. Do tell us, what do you say?'

At length all she could manage was a stammer. 'Your wish is mine too, Father.'

The old man had smiled. 'That will not do my dear. I cherish your opinion. Only if you really like him do you need to oblige.'

Shyly she had repeated: 'Yes, it is so father.'

Her consent was given. She felt she had spoken her heart. She liked the image of the young man who was to be her partner for life. Lean and fair, of healthy build, the Brahmin youth was undeniably handsome. His sensuous locks of unkempt hair and moustache framed a countenance that shone with radiance. But what captivated her most were the eyes. Those dark eyes that drew in everything in a compelling gaze. She could feel them on her, caressing her every inch as she stood by the doorway; it had made her hair stand on end. She was lost in reverie for a moment.

Durga had teased her, 'Learned pundit he may be but look at the way he has fallen for you. Hasn't he been stumped by your intelligence! Wait and see, his austere ways shall cower in your command. You are the end of all his searching. There'll be no realm outside the home for research and enquiry hereafter!'

Panchami took the remark lightly. Durga had always been an admirer, never saying a word to offend. 'But you flatter to deceive, Durga,' she had protested in earnest, even though Durga's reasoning intrigued her.

'I tend to think it was meant to be this way, Panchami. Doesn't the whole thing look like a happy coincidence of events? What else would explain the young man's coming on this auspicious day, the day that marks the ending of rituals for a favourable match for you? On completing the rites your father waited for a Brahmin to give away alms to, why ever would he insist so today?

'Then again wasn't it an unusual sight—an exhausted man lying by the ashoka tree early in the morning on our return from the river? You noticed the sacred thread across his chest, didn't you?' Durga persisted with a logic that was hard to dismiss. 'It was your recounting the incident to father that eventually brought him to our doorstep. Do you now see what I see?'

Panchami paused. The reconstruction of events had the feel of a carefully orchestrated drama. It was true, it was she who had seen the young man lying under the tree; she cast her mind back to the fateful morning of discovery. Early morning, dawn breaking in the woods as she made her way along the beaten path that led from the river. A dense silence hung in the air as she walked alone, Durga had stayed back by the riverbank for washing clothes. The path was a familiar one, along the riverside to its mouth by the cascade. Her steps trod certain, sure, to the bend by the ashoka tree. Suddenly she had stopped, her feet trembling. There, by the foot of the tree in the darkness of early morning, lay the body of a young man. Nearby were flung his staff and belongings knotted in a cloth. Dawn was just breaking in the skies overhead, the hazy light threw his form in a blur. She had stifled a cry and retreated backwards. Turning, she had run as fast as her legs could carry her. Dried leaves crackled under her feet, the woods vanished in a blinding haze as she had retraced her steps to the river. In her mind flashed a thought. What if… could it be…God no…that he was dead!

Mustering courage she had returned with Durga. Yes it was for real, there lay a motionless figure under the tree. But he had changed posture and now lay on his side. She noted the sacred white thread on his bare back. Panchami and Durga had exchanged a sigh of relief, the young man was alive after all. Must be a wandering ascetic who had chosen to rest awhile. Their fears allayed, they trod homeward. On reaching they had found Father at the steps. He had completed the rituals and was setting out in search of a Brahmin who could perform the rites that remained. Panchami informed him then that a poor Brahmin youth lay forlorn and exhausted under the tree near the river. She had begged her father to invite him home and offer alms. That would, she had insisted, be the most apt thing to do, the most benevolent gesture of worship on this auspicious day. Her heart went out to the young man, he seemed desolate. She had been stirred with sympathy.

In hindsight that had been the beginning. From compassion to respect to love, it had been a swift progression of affection. She shook her head unbelievingly. From the fateful encounter at dawn to the present; from sympathy to dejection, had her life really been a matter of choice?

*Durga was right, it was the hand of destiny that has lent me this state of mind, this maturity. This growth that has shackled me, body and mind. Twenty years of my life have I passed in marriage and so much has happened since. In a* detached rhythm, life has led me through motherhood not once, but eleven times. All abandoned by the wayside in the course of our journey. They all cried for an attention I could never give. A child with its mouth formed can well find its feed too, so reasons my scholarly husband. I was never one to argue nor even hold my own on behalf of my children. Meekly I obeyed in silent deference to his wishes. Time and again I have looked back with much regret. My life, my youth, my beliefs, everything I held dear have crumbled before my eyes. And yet nothing ever comes to an end in this marked existence, the same follies recur. Again, and again, and again.

Durga! How true of you to remind me of the hand of destiny then. I find myself now on a hillock. Wilderness all around, uninhabited as far as I can see. The cold comfort of a shelter woven of creepers and branches. Here I lie with the stirrings of another life within me, the pangs of another birth. A dutiful husband well-versed in life sciences lies in wait outside. A life is begotten anew, everything repeats.

# A Brother's Love

A hillock in the wilderness, remote and cast away from any sign of life. Here and there, vines and creepers have formed themselves into sheltering vaults that dot the expanse. The picture of desolation belied the advent of flowering. In one of the shelters there stirred the promise of a new life. Panchami was in the throes of another childbirth. Outside, a visibly tired Vararuchi stretched out in the shade of a tree. The waiting-in-attendance had become a familiar ritual now. This, the twelfth instance, found him lost deep in thought. The lines on his forehead spoke of long years of striving and conflict.

What was the nature of my striving, what changes had it wrought in me; little by little these riddles have answered themselves. There was once a time when I was angry, impatient; I was spoilt for prudence at a time when I needed it most. Our first child… the abandoning at birth… I was beside myself with rage then, my stubbornness knew no bounds. Am I the very one that walked away in an uncontrollable fit then? He wondered aloud in startled disbelief. The lessons life had taught hadn't been small, nor minor were the changes time had wrought.

But there remained a truth, an abject one he had taught himself. Of the sanctity of human feeling, its unquestionable legitimacy that lent a glow to the living. Beyond mind, beyond measure, the realization stood with all the conviction of an infallible truth. Yet it had been no easy tide that had led him until here. The tortuous passage spoke of many a sacrifice and tests of endurance. To arrive at this, his port of calling; a harbour to dock his conscience on.

My face, my features…did you find a change in me? A weariness, a guilt? No. A change, perhaps, but certainly not of guilt. And why ever would you? Yours but to do your duty without fretting about the result, those were the words of the wise. Countless have been the brickbats I have fended along the way. Cruel, unfeeling, inhuman, many such unflattering epithets have I heard to my name. A father who could never spare any affection for his children, a sinner indeed. But I was never one to be taken up with these trifles. The nature of my calling made extreme demands of my worldly obligations. A dispassionate weighing of life and death becomes inevitable at times. Understandably, one's motives aren't always clear. Given the circumstances, the best of actions appear ill-intentioned. One's motives may seem dubious, one's prerogatives mistaken. Yes, that has been a tragedy I've had to live with…my own brother was no exception, he too misunderstood me. And to have thought that we would never meet again…it had been an entirely unexpected event.

\*\*\*

Vararuchi stood at the court of the king of Kulasekhara, expounding on his study of the astronomical calendar, the Panchangam. Facing him and hanging on to every word of his was a sea of scholars, who had come from far and wide. For Vararuchi, the people gathered were but a multitude, a necessary prop to showcase his brilliance. He addressed no one in particular. The sea of faces blurred indistinctly into each other. All of a sudden, a form from their midst swam into focus. In a passing gaze he discerned someone in a corner. There must have been something that caught the eye, he thought, as he noted a tonsured head and saffron robes. A flicker of familiarity perhaps. He jerked his gaze and lingered on the form that had caught his attention. An instant was all it took. Those searching eyes, that beauty of countenance—Brother! He stood dumbfounded, how the recognition had come flooding from a forgotten chapter of his past! It was so many years since they had been separated; he had doubted the possibility of their ever meeting again. Was he alive at all, the last he had heard of brother had been of his hasty flight to Nepal. He shuddered. Nepal, the dreaded land of lore, of cannibals, of men sacrificed at the evil altar. He had had a vision once—of Brother at a ritual sacrifice in the company of bloodthirsty warriors, in a temple of the dead. That brother should find himself in such sinful company, he trembled at the thought. The fear had remained forever inside of him, the embers smouldering on a low fire. It had continued to haunt him, darkening his nights with nightmarish visions of blood and gore. To see his brother now, in such a circumstance, in an appearance of gentility...he was too stunned for words.

His voice trailed into silence. Turning to the King, Vararuchi pleaded, 'Your majesty, allow me to pause for now, I shall continue a little while later.'

Surprised by the turn of events, the King enquired concernedly, 'What is it, Vararuchi, any cause for uneasiness?'

Vararuchi stammered, half-turning to the King, his eyes glued to his brother. 'I can't go on, I can see my brother in the audience.' His voice broke, 'A brother I had lost when I was a child, whom I never thought would meet again ever.' His eyes spoke of their bereavement. The King followed Vararuchi's gaze, where it lay unwavering.

'The man in saffron? Why, he is none other than Dharmapadar, a Buddhist monk of renown!'

Vararuchi's eyes widened in disbelief. 'Buddhist? Dharmapadar, who?'

The King explained, 'Yes, the saint Dharmapadar. We have invited him to convene an assembly of world religions tomorrow.'

But Vararuchi was not convinced. 'It's my brother for sure. I take leave of your Majesty; let me go up to him.'

Vararuchi waded into the audience hurriedly. The monk in saffron smiled steadily. His face betrayed not a trace of surprise or recognition. It was a perfunctory smile, disarming in its simplicity, which bore neither affection nor malice. Vararuchi advanced. As he drew closer the still smiling monk gathered himself on his wooden sandals.

'Yes Vararuchi, what made you stop so? I had come to witness your eloquence.'

It was as natural as though they had met but yesterday. The smile that played on his lips held not a trace of mockery. The air of disaffection had given way to tenderness and compassion. A loving fondness marked his features, before him stood the brother who had so lovingly raised him as a child. He reached out and held him in a tight embrace. The years of separation, of struggle, of seeking had come a full circle at last. At length he stepped back and looked Vararuchi carefully from head to toe. In his mind was the image of the hard-working, innocent boy that he once knew. 'A long way you have come my dear little brother, a long way indeed.'

Vararuchi hadn't overcome his surprise yet. 'What brings you here, brother?'

'Doesn't my appearance make it obvious? I'm here for a meeting of world religions. I'm actually on my way to the Sinhala kingdom to take part in a ritual undertaking. It was on alighting here that I learnt of your discourse, as my good fortune would have it. I had always wanted to attend one as I have heard a great deal of you for so long.'

Heard a great deal, what had he heard? Touched to the quick as though in anticipation of a reproach, Vararuchi retorted: 'Hearsay can often be unpleasant.'

'Pleasant or unpleasant, good or bad, aren't these relative judgements? What's good for one might be bad for another. Likewise, what's bad for one could be seen as good for the other. Let that be, you do seem rather tired and weary.'

It was a rhetoric that was lost on the younger brother. Vararuchi was feverishly contemplating everything of his past that his brother might have heard about. The divide in their pursuits since their parting at childhood would, he imagined, throw up awkward questions of right and wrong. It disconcerted him a little that the bittersweet circumstance of their reunion held the portents of a confrontation. And hence the relief he felt that Panchami was not with him at the moment. His predicament and his confusion remained well hidden from her.

They walked in silence along the dried bed of the Thiruvanchikulam River. It was late evening and the sun was setting on the distant shore. The patch of shrubbery that guarded the shrine of the serpents was silhouetted against the reddening sky. As it descended into the horizon, the diminishing crescent lent a touch of gold to the edges in the scenery. Its gentle rays caressed the long-lost brothers in an affectionate afterglow. They walked along the sands of the long dried riverbed. Beneath their feet, the damp white sand gave way with a soft squish. The riverbed was dotted with the imprint of two pairs of feet that trod side by side in measured steps. Here and there, the water had found its way in thin trickles, little rivulets dancing as they snaked their path in the sand. Overhead, the birds were calling it a day, heading homeward to roost in noisy flocks. The air hung heavy with the weight of years that separated them. Their early years together in a troubled childhood seemed far removed from the present. It rendered them, in effect, two people unknown to each other but for a distant memory, who had drifted so far apart in thought and action as to have become strangers.

At length, the elder brother looked Vararuchi in the eye and spoke, 'Tell me then, all of yourself...'

Vararuchi was momentarily perplexed. The searching eyes fell on him with all the force of a blow. What had he to say? Looking back he saw his endeavour as a tale of unfulfilled promise, all the subject of wishful thinking. One who had wished to become a scholar. One who had felt, painfully so, the urge to question the sciences. One who had sought to force the hand of destiny and unravel new grounds of thought and action for mankind. But what had actually transpired? The unfolding of events conveyed almost a sense of surrender. The self-proclaimed ascetic hadn't reached anywhere in his chosen path. From the pedestal of high intent to the reality of the present, the descent was as humbling as it was unsettling. On the tree of knowledge he had shaken and scoured every branch, yet none had yielded a clue. His reply held more than a trace of guilt: 'Nothing has happened really, my research and experimentation go on.'

He would have wished to add that all was smooth sailing, even that he had chanced upon some progress here and there. But that would not be the truth. The truth was altogether different and harsh. He had realized that his quest had become more arduous by the day. His willpower was not what it used to be. He felt more and more removed from the world around him....But his pride prevented him from admitting this.

'Ah, so you are still in the course of your wanderings...'

His brother would have deliberately skirted any mention of Panchami and children. He himself was reluctant to touch upon it. Carefully he replied, 'What you call wandering is to me enquiry.'

'You are running after that which does not exist, is that what you call enquiry? Vararuchi! God knows fate has been unkind to us innocents. Our childhood was bleak, early in life we were tossed up and down by this hostile world. Our coming of age was a lesson in survival. You might not know all the scars I've borne in my travels, you needn't either. Somehow, through all of it, I've found my shore. I've arrived at my port of calling and found my truth. To me you are still a child, the helpless brother I had left all alone. Tell me, your elder brother who loves you more than words can say, why do you suffer so? And what of those who are your own, have you no regard for their feelings?'

*I find no reason to doubt the sincerity of his feelings. But am I to give in? Unto each his own.* 'I need no advice from anyone, my brother even. My truth is mine alone.' There was an edge to Vararuchi's voice now. The trademark arrogance had crept into his voice. Or was it the distance of all these years that gave him this haughtiness? Icily, he continued, 'I certainly am not suffering. Nor am I causing anyone else to suffer. Very simply, I lead my life the way I choose to. Perhaps it is not to the taste of a Buddhist monk.'

He looked sidelong at his brother and was defeated by his composure. The benign smile had died on his lips. The serene eyes held deep sympathy and disapproval. His brother said, 'When you live life on your own terms, what of those who are with you? What of the pain that you bring to them? Do you care for the woman who grieves for your love and is alone in her suffering? Who, even as we stand here, is being wasted, in body and mind? Why, it is a terrible plight even we monks can see and feel.'

Vararuchi listened, taken aback. So this was it, he felt betrayed. Brother had come armed with hearsay and rumour. And that could never be flattering. He was disenchanted. It appeared that battle lines had been drawn for a confrontation. Resignedly, he said, 'You would have heard a great deal of me and my mistakes. Let's not discuss that. Let's not pick an argument now, I'm so glad that we've met after all these years.'

In spite of his words he half expected an argument to ensue but was again disarmed by his brother's reaction. His brother's face softened, a serenity marked his features. It radiated a peace that only an abiding faith could give. Vararuchi stared in confusion. The point of his reasoning was confounded by this man and his composure. The two men, brothers by birth but strangers by circumstance, were a study in contrasts. One a hardened rationalist that trod on the unforgiving path of logic and reason; the other a seasoned believer, a man of faith and love. Unable to understand each other, they stood divided by the divergent paths they had chosen.

'Dear child! I can never bring myself to quarrel with you. You are my younger brother, the child whom Mother and

Father entrusted me with. I could never look after you the way I should have. But your fame was far reaching, and many a time did I try to meet you. This visit here too, is just so that I could see you.' Like a sage, he continued, his tone brooking neither dissent nor argument: 'Vararuchi! Your face speaks of untold unhappiness and ill-health. It is a wearying path that you tread; uncertain, unsure of the outcome. Success or failure, you do not yourself know. This is not something you can solve through wit or mere tactic alone. The truth is to be won over not by conquest but by detachment. Indeed, there should be no victory or defeat in this endeavour, for it is the ego that hungers for victory every time. From ego to desire and from desire to dissatisfaction is but a swift and inevitable progression. Try to detach yourself from the outcome. You will arrive at the truth. Happiness and fulfilment will be yours. In the end, you will realize that love is everything.'

His voice grew grim. 'This is the word of a defeated man, one that his younger brother would do well to understand.' His face softened into a smile.

Vararuchi tried to match his brother's assurance with a weak smile. Deep inside, the words had touched a chord in his troubled soul. 'I could not be like you,' his voice broke. 'Try as I might...'

'But why ever would you try?' Brother's voice rose with feeling. 'No, never, this is never expected of you. Be yourself, that will do.' His voice deepened with emphasis, 'Your own self, your own man. The vast expanse of the human soul is yours to conquer, then will you realize yourself. The desire for revenge, the urge to settle scores is an exercise in wastefulness that will lead you nowhere.'

The fire in his eyes was searing and matched the fervour of his voice. The bloodshot eyes called to Vararuchi's mind the memory of a gruesome vision.

'But do you remember who had sown the seed of revenge in me?' Vararuchi reproached him.

Silence. All the pain, the tumult of their early years, flashed before Brother's mind. The passing away of their mother and the misery in its wake, the plight of two innocent children left to fend for themselves. A grief-stricken younger brother she had left in his care. He had had to console him, was duty bound to fulfil expectations. The hour of adversity had brought with it the seeds of their own undoing. At length he replied quietly, 'But that was then, Vararuchi. We have come a long way since then haven't we? We now understand that the vengeful instinct poisons the mind. That the germ of the ego it breeds ultimately destroys. Aren't we now the wiser for our mistakes?'

It was a disarming argument that left Vararuchi at a loss. The silvery white of the riverbed was speckled with a touch of red. The brothers sat on the bank, their legs playing idly on a little patch of water in the sand. The river had long ceased to flow, there remained but a dampness that recalled the rain of yesterday. Here and there the ebb of the river had settled into little puddles of a muddy brown. A dank odour of moss rose from the marshlike bed of the river. Woven into it was the dense silence between the brothers. It hung heavy and suffocating, a vacant presence in the late evening air. Almost on cue, the cool air that wafted over them lost its composure some and broke into a cold sweat. And there crept in uninvited, memories of the past; painful, unsettling episodes of hardship and endurance. Vararuchi looked sidelong at his brother. The moon shone bright as ever through the summer haze. Vararuchi could detect a certain melancholy beneath the serenity that illuminated his brother. The bearing was noble, the air distant, unreachable, as though the work of an accomplished hand in solid marble. But for an agonized memory Vararuchi could never have recognized him as the brother he knew. The brother he remembered had seemed all too human, in gaiety, in anger, in mirth. But the figure before him seemed lonely, too soon grown old. Since their parting what would he have endured to age thus? His heart went out to his brother as he thought of the trials and tribulations time must have wrought on his sensitive nature.

'You might not know…you needn't either…' What was that he had said of his travails? One thing he was certain of—the brother he knew had long since ceased to exist. Perhaps devoured by a cannibal, irrevocably altered, irredeemably lost to himself and those he held dear. The tonsured sage that stood before him was a complete stranger. There was not a trace of the vulnerability that had once marked him. Did he carry the faintest recollection of his past life? Vararuchi felt a twinge for the brother he had known, for the man he had been. The breach in time was irreconcilable and filled the vacant silence between them. At length, the elder one spoke,

'Well, what do you derive from your seeking? Where does your pursuit lead you?'

Vararuchi looked keenly. For a moment he thought it was a rebuke. But no, brother would have long lost any sense of irony or humour. He was genuinely anxious to know. Vararuchi delved into himself for an answer. The question was deceptively simple, the answer not quite so. He heard himself saying. 'A greater vigour for life, a release from all this desolation.'

He halted abruptly, that was all he could say. The two exchanged long, searching glances. As though appraising each other, measuring the distance the years had created. Time certainly hasn't dimmed his personality, thought Vararuchi. Notwithstanding a clean-shaven pate and the weight of years behind him, he was yet an image of masculinity. It was impossible to fathom the thoughts that lay beneath the benign exterior.

Presently he spoke, 'Your reply is what one would expect of any self-centred person. Rather the logic of one who's taken to drink.'

His tone was measured but there was no mistaking the incisiveness. 'Vararuchi! You are beyond doubt intelligent and able. But that ought not to be a self-indulgent end in itself. Its true value lies in the joy it can bring to others. The spirit of revenge that guides your pursuit can never bring fulfilment. Love alone endures. One who shuns it is the poorer for its absence. For he is not blessed with the compassion that it brings and which paves the way to lasting fulfilment. Your enquiry is well in its place and so is your vaulting ambition. But remember, it is a mother's instinct that you stifle, her tender heart that bleeds in the course of your seeking. For sure, one cannot hope to any attainment by being indifferent to that. It is a path to a bad end that you tread.'

Vararuchi sat listening, shocked into numbness. His brother's words had hit at the mark of a long forgotten wound. He felt a great weariness. This stranger, whom he had once called brother and his words of foreboding, had reawakened in him a near-buried memory. He could well have turned away then and there, but was drawn in spite of himself to the man and his words. He peered into his brother's luminous eyes and sensed a deep sorrow in his gaze. In his bearing was manifest the ache of a lifetime, on his countenance was the cast of a long and troubled past. The path to deliverance had indeed been tortuous.

'It is from the shackles of the self that one needs to break free. Overcome desire and vanity. You'll discover that the means and the ends are but one, for a life that resonates with the Truth.' His brother's voice continued in a sage-like monotone that Vararuchi was beginning to tire of, but he kept silent, wondering how much this man would have endured in his time.

'Perhaps,' his brother appeared to be speaking to himself, 'it is in the nature of truth that it unfolds unto each in its own way. If you were to know how it happened to me…'

Brother sighed, as Vararuchi continued listening in disbelief. 'I had fled from home to make good my escape to faraway Nepal. But as ill luck would have it, I fell into the hands of the guardsmen at the Kali Ghats. A Brahmin, a man of God—how could they possibly kill me? So they chose for me an alternative: I was made factotum to the chief priest. I had no choice, among fiends bound to further their fiendish ends. My being a Brahmin had saved me from a certain death, only to leave me more vulnerable than ever. I was to learn that a more gruesome fate awaited me.

'It was rumoured that the land and its people were under an evil eye. The guardian deity had to be propitiated, and a life to be sacrificed. I remember that fateful night, the fifth of the new moon, it was the month of Ashweena. A young man from a distant land was brought bound and gagged. The pitiful soul was to become an unfortunate scapegoat in the occult mission. The revelry that began late evening went into the early hours of the next day. All night long the devils sang and danced around the campfire, in sadistic anticipation of the act. The object of their rapture, the innocent man stood forlorn and withering, his agony mounting as the hours passed. Before his eyes was the ghastly parade that seemed headed to a certain climax. And by his side, knife in hand, standing guard, was I. It was difficult to say who was the more helpless one, the more dispossessed: he, a prisoner of fate who stood resigned to his end, or I, trapped in a circumstance that I had no choice but to accept. Fear, bewilderment, panic, and a desperate urge to break free tore at my heart. The goings-on around me were a blur, the din and hustle numbed my senses.'

'As the appointed hour inched near, I was seized with conflict. The slightest sign of dissent would spell my doom. And mute acceptance would make me an accomplice to this ghastly act of murder! With all my heart, I entreated my saviour that my life be spared of this sin. Even as I prayed silently, around me the frenzied pounding continued. Past midnight and into the wee hours of the morning it wore on. The proposed hour was nigh at hand when, suddenly, a rumble was heard in the thicket. As though in answer to my prayer, it seemed deliverance was in sight. I heard a beating of drums to the accompaniment of a whooping war cry. The darkness was illumined by flaming torches that appeared to have sprung from nowhere. It was an ambush by the captive youth's brethren. They swooped as one on the unsuspecting natives; a bloody melee ensued. My heart beat fast. What was I to do, I had no sides to take, no loyalties either way. As I hesitated the conflict intensified. And in the confusion I broke free. Running as fast as my feet could carry me, I tore into the heart of the abounding thicket. The clang of metal and the cry for blood rang in my ears. Soon, I came upon a thick bush by the trunk of a tree. I hid in its cover. In the distance the clash continued, the darkness dotted with the light from torches held aloft by the invaders. As I waited for an opportune moment to move, I heard a hurried shuffle. Short quick footsteps that came closer and closer, and a panting! Someone was running towards me! With a start I drew my executioner's knife and stepped out. In the hazy light of dawn I saw a blur of red.'

'In a blood red robe clinging to him, beads glistening around his neck—the very outfit of the sacrificial prey—was the young prisoner. One of his men had set him free. In an instant he froze in his tracks, half retreating. The sight of me, knife in hand, must have been gruesome. He saw in me an enemy whose motive he did not quite understand. I was to him one among them with no intent but to kill. Seeing death in the face and his newfound liberation abruptly cut short, he flailed his arms in dismay.'

'"If so be my fate…but tell me for once, what wrong have I done you, Sir, to deserve this wretched end?"'

'The import of his words was lost on me. I was no less taken aback than he at our encounter. All I perceived was a pitiful cry, a plea for reason. My heart went out to him. Hastily I beckoned him near so that he may take cover beside me. "Fast my friend, crawl over here quick," I whispered to him.'

'Scarce had I uttered these words that the young man's eyes widened; a look as though of disbelief swam in those eyes, and with a thud he fell face forward to the ground. He had been felled by a captor's lance. I rushed to his side and raised his face. The rapier point had cut through his nape and exited from the front. It was a fatal blow and his life was ebbing. I laid him on my lap and looked into those eyes. In those last faltering moments, he raised his eyes and with an effort held me in his gaze. I felt he recognized me through his pain. His voice quivered, his speech was slurred. "But what wrong did I ever do you…what have I done to deserve this…"'

'His voice trailed away into emptiness, before I knew it was all over.'

Vararuchi looked closer at his brother. The sage-like visage now looked all too human; the eyes were brimming with tears.

'The poor soul that passed away on my lap did not know my predicament, that his slaying was not of my doing. I will never forget the look of reproach in his eyes. As the light died out in them, the look of bafflement remained. I lay there, faint with the dead man's weight on my knee. When I came back to my senses I was at a Buddha Vihara where Sage Tathagatha was. In my mouth was the aftertaste of sin, the lump in my throat tasted of blood. On my mind weighed a terrible guilt — of a deed I had been witness to, one I had abetted. A dark stain coursed through me, poisoning me all over. I kept thinking, if the youth's kinsmen had not come to his rescue, it would've been my hands that wielded the axe. Ever since, the fifth day of the month of Ashweena is a day I cannot bring myself to forget. His last words echoed in me: "But what wrong did I ever do you…"

'The fragility of life, its preciousness, came home to me then, Vararuchi! It is not in our hands to resurrect a life. And in like measure, not ours to take one either. The incident left in me an ache that I have not been able to forget. Never before, nor since, have I felt such grief. My whole being seemed a wasted wreck, edging to slow ruin. In the man that lay struck by the fatal blow, reeling in a pool of blood, I saw myself—me in the darkness of doubt, despair, and vengeance. I prayed for an end to my torment.'

*Let this earth swallow me,*
*Or let me be reduced to ashes.*

'I was convinced that no ordinary power on earth could save me from this crisis of conscience. I was certain that it would take a divine intervention, a momentous one. "My saviour, where are you?" my helplessness found a voice that was as shrill as it was desperate. "Are you listening? Believe me, it was not I that killed the boy, will you convey this to the poor soul? Oh, free me from this guilt."'

' When I came to my senses, I was on the lap of Sage Tathagatha. My weary eyelids opened to meet a serene gaze, I felt the caress of a passing breeze.'

'"Arise, son! It is not for you to take a life...what has passed is not of your doing." His words carried the quiet conviction of a truth I recognized instinctively. The bearded visage looked at me steadily; to look into those eyes was to know peace. I felt a stirring within, a sense of awakening had begun to dawn. I realized that my search had come to an end. I was face to face with the overpowering beauty, the force of Truth. All my wrongs came undone in that moment of liberation; I recognized my saviour Bodhisattva.'

Vararuchi's brother fell silent, his face showed neither sorrow nor triumph. From agony to ecstasy it had been a pilgrim's progress come full circle. An uneasy silence fell between them. The weight of years sat lightly between them, the memory of past hardships was a silent presence. The cool night air made as though to forget the misfortunes of past years. In a weary descent they sank into the soft riverbed.

Overhead, the moon shone on them. The younger one looked searchingly at his long-lost brother. Across the riverbank, an eerie quietness had cast a long shadow.

*Whither the gulf, was it not of your making? A trick of time more imagined than real, a mirage the years that separated you and me.'*

In like measure, the ill-fated night of the full moon had marked their lives. Hapless, they found themselves on the losing side, battling a force of circumstance beyond their control. No, the sense of estrangement between them was only an illusion. The cross they bore, their destinies that ran parallel to each other, linked them more than they realized. Vararuchi was overcome with feeling. Between the sage and the seeker was a kinship as old as time. There now remained no barrier of the self, nor of consciousness. Each was transparent, a window unto the other. Achingly, Vararuchi murmured: 'Always my brother, for ever.'

Presently they rose. The evening hour was late. A breeze swayed the boughs of the willow overhead. Stray flowers drifted in the air, at the mercy of the passing wind, finally fluttering to rest on the soft sand of the riverbed. Gathering Vararuchi close to him, Brother spoke, 'The light will doubtless come to you, Vararuchi—the light of love, of compassion. If not now, then in some time. My prayers for my little one shall not go unheard. All your sins, the shadows you've cast in your earnest seeking, shall all be quelled by the power of prayer.' With a pause, he continued, 'The light of Truth shall shine on you. And when it does, you'll know no worry, no desire, no sorrow...'

Vararuchi was too overwhelmed to speak. Nestled in his brother's embrace he felt like a little boy again. In a flash, the riverbank faded, the years behind them vanished. They were frolicking together in a long-gone childhood summer, playing marbles, splashing about in the river.

'I haven't met your wife, where is she?' The question was abrupt, simple. The question was expected, of course, and Vararuchi replied in the manner of one who had prepared a ready answer: 'She is with child, resting at the guest quarters, I couldn't bring her along.' There it ended; no probing queries: how many children, no niceties about her health, nothing. Brother was remarkably restrained.

Late at night, they reached the quarters where Panchami lay resting. His brother saw her for the first time. He lay his hands on her head and blessed her. His words were affectionate, more a suggestion to Vararuchi: 'You both are no longer children now, dear one. Put an end to the wanderlust, settle down at some place. Do not forget that from this generation to the next, it is through you that the family line passes.' He bid farewell with the words, 'We shall meet again someday.'

Early next morning they parted—his brother to the kingdom of Sinhala, Vararuchi to the discourse at Thaliyaathiri.

# The Newborn's Silence

'I'm tired…can't bring myself to…' Panchami faltered as they approached a hillock on the way to the shrine at Thaliyaathiri. Vararuchi turned, looking closely. The pangs of another birth? But surely, it was too early to feel the pain yet.

'A premature birth!' His mind raced to the eventuality, and for once the distant words found utterance on his lips: 'Oh God!'

Hurriedly he sought a shelter in the overgrowth. The hillock was dotted with creepers and vines. Here and there, their arms arched and meshed in a dense envelope of twigs, branches, and dried leaves. Within them was a cosy recess, a natural chamber welcoming and protective. The rough-hewn floor he covered with a soft quilt of leaves. Set within the caring confines of nature, the serendipitous dwelling was ready for a new arrival. Gently, he laid her on the soft ground and stepped outside. Vararuchi stood outside, waiting for the cry of the newborn. His eyes were moist; his manner betrayed a vulnerability that would have surprised his followers. Beneath the world-weary exterior of the man of wisdom there lurked a restlessness, a wishing for what could have been. Had he not shied away from the responsibility of a husband, had he welcomed the children that came and went...so many harsh choices, so many regrets. In quieter moments such as this the past stole into him, unsettling his certainty. Had he, had he not, had he, had... The argument was a hopeless one, a relentless tug of war between the heart and the head. *All my victories came at a great price. If I have pursued my goal with singular devotion, ignoring the call of human bondage, then I've also known the pain of isolation that accompanied it. If I stepped clear of the entanglement of kinships, it was a sacrifice I knowingly made. To the world I was Vararuchi, scholar-scientist who would let no hurdle come in the path of right action. My detractors called me cold and unfeeling, but I was never one to bother.*

Until now. 'Love alone endures. One who shuns it is the poorer for its loss. For he is not blessed with the compassion that it brings, which paves the way to lasting fulfilment...' Brother's words rang in his ears. It was a counterpoint he had heard before. Time and again, it had raised its head in dissent and he had borne it with discomfiture. Loud, vociferous, almost indisputable in its certainty, it was a voice he recognized as his own, come from his alter ego. Over and over he turned it over in his mind, and found his thoughts converging. The argument had found its mark. Brother had always been right.

'Panchami!' he implored silently, 'for once if you could...' He found himself yearning that she would beg of her own accord—'just this once, let him be, grant me my motherhood.' A look, a gesture, was all who would ever need. That in answer to her plea he could indulge himself in that blissful moment of forgetting when the child would be in his arms, the face upturned to his, to kiss it but once, to feel the warmth of the little one against his own.

But the unspoken wish was to go unrequited; Panchami had steeled herself against her unfortunate circumstance. That first instance, her heart in her mouth as she begged of him had been her last. Ever since, she had never yielded to emotion. One by one she had foregone the births with not a whimper of protest. Silent in sacrifice, she remained ever the dutiful wife, the unflinching ally to her husband's will. A long, loving kiss before parting was all she bequeathed her children before the decisive moment. Fighting tears and the urge to turn back, she hung behind him doggedly, a witless ghost, a hapless shadow in his unremitting quest.

*My little ones… what of them?*

*Are they well, wherever they be?*

*Would each know the other, were they to meet…?*

Her tortured mind preyed on these questions that had no answer. But the mother's kiss carried the blessing of life, and she was certain that her children would endure. But that was poor recompense for her misery, the scars of a lifetime remained.

The stage was set for the twelfth child-to-be, everything the same as before. She writhed in pain in the wilderness, he lay in wait by the shade of a tree outside.

What was to come of this? Was this child to meet a similar fate as its siblings? Was he to go the way of his siblings before?

But no, the resolute seeker has had a change of mind; though he didn't have the humility to admit it.

*For once if only she would plead my consent, I would gladly agree.*

So with calculated indifference, he paced about under the shade. But his stoical calm was missing; he paused many a time at the opening of the chamber.

*Where was the familiar cry?*

His feet carried him to the very threshold, only to turn away in dogged determination.

*Isn't it well near the time?*

All his defences faltered; his apprehension defied him. At long length he cried out, his voice an undisguised appeal: 'Panchami! Why does the child not cry?'

From within comes the mournful repartee, 'He can't, how could he…his mouth isn't formed.'

Vararuchi froze, unbelieving. The reply stung him into silence, shaking at the very foundation of his being. The carefully constructed defences of his world shook and crumbled to dust. In his eyes was a faraway look. The mighty Vararuchi's eyes were brimming over; the storm raging within him ready to break any moment. Slowly, he raised himself, the weary traveller in an unending quest, wreathed in doubt and remorse. The days and nights of wanderlust had left him no wiser than at the beginning. In fact, it had been an exercise in futility. Staggering to the doorstep of the shelter he peered inside, unbelieving. His eyes met Panchami's. She was faint with fatigue and weeping. Her one arm held close in an inseparable embrace the frigid body of their child. His gaze fell on the diminutive, lifeless form beside her; it was the first time he had brought himself to look at his child. It was true, the child had no mouth. Panchami looked at him keenly: 'We don't have to cast him away, do we?"

It was the reproach of a wounded mother at the end of her tether. Vararuchi could not but submit in resignation. He made no attempt to conceal. He had thrown away the elaborate cloak of learning; what remained was grief—profound and helpless.

Quietly, in grim acceptance he said, 'I had wished you would take exception to my word and insist on keeping the child this time.'

Panchami wept uncontrollably, she had come to the end of her resilience. 'My mind was set on this one, come what may. Curse me, disown me, or kill me if you will, I wouldn't have flinched. Never was I going to let go the child. And now...'

Vararuchi was at a loss for words. Had he been marked by the perverse irony of fate yet again?

'Oh, I am but a plaything in the hands of destiny!'

Panchami did not understand, the import of her husband's words was beyond her. 'But...but what wrong have I done?' Her question was all innocence, lost in the tragedy of the moment.

His eyes brimming with tears, Vararuchi regarded the dead body of his son. He gathered him in his arms and stroked him gently as though he were alive.

'My dear son, my child! You have passed to immortality, leaving this wretch undeserving of any more than a lifeless child. But your heart beats with mine, our lives are one forever. In me is a life for you to live to the fullest. Grant me this, even if only as an imagined thing.'

Panchami started, what was she hearing? For a moment her distress was forgotten. 'Good heavens, is this the Vararuchi I knew? A transformation indeed, we are blessed! Has he become an ordinary man at last?'

Vararuchi turned to her, his words pouring out in the manner of a prophecy: 'Panchami, this child of ours is no ordinary one, he is destined for greatness. All the endowments and glories his father sought but could never have shall be his. My erudition, all my strength, flows from me to his body. We shall bury him here in the hillock. Tomorrow his name will reach far and wide as the Lord of the Hill without a Mouth. Everything around us will be touched with his divinity.'

Pausing he added, 'As for me, I remain an ordinary man, in worship of our godly son. I shall spend my days in prayer atoning for my sins.'

With a heavy heart, Vararuchi lifted the body of the lifeless child and laid him on the grassy meadow. The forehead of the mound he creased with a gash that ran deep and wide into the hillock. He laid the body of the child to rest inside and began filling the opening with mud. Soon the surface was level with the mound, the little one lay buried in the hillock. He gathered pebbles from here and there, and placed them into the muddy surface. The dead child's grave was marked on the hill with a floor of pebbles.

The act of burial done, Vararuchi laid a weary head to the grave. The sobs were heavy, uncontrollable, and held the anguish of an inconsolable father. From inside him a voice cried out. 'Dear son, God knows your father has been humbled many a time by the hand of fate. The reversal this time has cost him dear, but is not entirely in vain. In my defeat lies the impetus to your success. Yours to come all glories, all strength...'

But wait, what was it that sounded in the silence of the late evening? He listened carefully, turning an ear to the wind; it seemed to come from inside the hollow where he lay. At first faintly, then slowly rising in shrillness, it rang clear and piercing. The heart-rending clarion call of a newborn signalling its arrival into the world. As he listened, the wailing grew louder and louder; it was not one, not two, not three but many voices that echoed in unison from the dark hollow. Twelve children, twelve lost souls in the first flush of their coming, crying for attention, an affection that was never to be. In the stillness of the night the hillock and its enveloping wilderness resounded with the shrill, tearful cries of the twelve. Louder and louder the chorus rose, echoing darkly in the confines of the hollow. Vararuchi collapsed by the graveside, overwhelmed by voices from the past, a painful persistent reminder of his folly.

Panchami watched, bewildered. In her imagination she saw her twelve little ones before her eyes. All around the grassy mound they were gathered, their cries merging into one another, a shrill crowd demanding her attention. 'Mother, oh Mother!' The cries pounded at the doors of her conscience. For long had she steeled herself from the instincts of motherhood, now she would bear it no more. Her defences gave way, she advanced feebly towards her children but found her legs weakening. Her legs buckled as she tumbled to the ground beside Vararuchi.

With a start, Vararuchi awoke to find her by his side. He held out a firm hand and made her rise. It was a rare moment of closeness; her upturned eyes met his and held him steadily. Never before had she looked him in the eye. It was a gaze that held a world of unspoken feeling. There was love mixed with anger, malice mingled with self-pity, but above all a reproach, a silent reprimand. Vararuchi quailed before her, his face ashen with shame and guilt.

Quick to perceive, Panchami lowered her eyes and spoke: 'It has been the lot of women to endure thus. From the beginning of time, she has been discredited as weak and infirm. My harsh apprenticeship under the mighty Vararuchi has only proved the myth to be true. Here I stand, frail of body and mind, a weakling unable to stand on my own.'

Her manner and tone belied the resignation in her words. It was even, detached without a hint of reproach. 'But it pains me to see the wise Vararuchi suffer so. That he who had subdued me should himself weaken so. Are we really better off for the sacrifices we have made?'

She turned to look at the mound where he had buried the child. There lay her children, all twelve of them, crying. Hastily, she let go of Vararuchi's arm and moved towards her children. Head bent in prayer on the stone floor she cried: 'Forgive me, my little ones. Forgive your mother her frailties. I never had the strength nor the will when I needed it. My love for you was always a heartless one.'

Head bowed on the stone, her body convulsing in sobs, she continued, 'Your father too failed to show me the way. Dear children, I turn to you, give me the courage, the will I never had.'

Vararuchi did not intervene in her grief. Silently he stood as she gave full rein to her sorrow; it was the unburdening of a lifetime of hardship and sacrifice. At length, as her cries subsided he came near and reminded her gently, 'Our crying by the graveside at this hour is a bad omen. It bodes not well for the departed soul that rests here.'

Each holding the other, they made their way down the hillside. Silhouetted against the fading evening light, the weary scholar and his frail wife were a picture of desolation. Their shadows lengthened as they descended the slope. Soon, it was night. Their shadows melted into the darkness as their forms grew fainter in the fading light.

# A Challenge and Hope

A deserted village shrouded in silence and an unchecked wilderness. Every step, every turn spurred a memory. Waves gently lapped at the steps by the water's edge, at the secluded bathing ghat of Panchami's childhood. The regular slabs of stone had splintered and leaned precariously into the water. Feet could no longer find its way in the slippery moss; the old clearing was now a thicket overgrown with shrubbery and brambles. Not far away was a crumbling monument, a remnant of what was once a living presence. The shrine of evening prayer was in ruins. An air of desolation and loss hung like a pall over the village. If but the stones could speak what ghastly tales would they recount? Of marauders, barbarians come on a spree, of death, destruction and loss in their wake, perhaps. What horrors lay behind the wreckage, one would never know. Time in desperate disguise had done the inevitable, the dense overgrowth did well to conceal in its folds the scars of ruin.

Panchami and Vararuchi found themselves where they had begun; their wandering had come a full circle. Was it the hand of fate that concluded the years of dogged pursuit in a retracing of steps that shaped such an unlikely homecoming? And what remained of home after all—Father whom she well knew not to expect, nor friends or kin… a face flashed into memory. Durga! She sighed, but how could it be? A hard life had wiped out all traces of kith or kin. She imagined the tranquil place and its people under the shadow of the ruthless marauders. Fleeing for life under cover of darkness and the wilderness, the few lucky ones who had managed to survive would have made good their escape. Those that remained…she shuddered to think of their end.

So that was it, the end of all she knew, all she held dear, Panchami reflected achingly. No reassuring faces, none to look forward to—how was she to carry on? The years stretched ahead long, lonely, and remote. Her steps led her from the water's edge to where her home once stood. There was the ashoka tree, now older, still by the wayside. And by its foot she thought she saw a young man, faint with exhaustion, fast asleep. It was a memory so ancient that it appeared almost imagined—that trembling moment of meeting, that momentous crossing at dawn. She paused, drawn to the memory of the past. Resting her head to its trunk, she sat by the tree, her heart heavy. By her side lay Vararuchi, resting his head by the foot of the tree. It was a moment borrowed from history, a telling likeness from a time long ago. Ah, but how time had altered them! A thin, shrivelled body, flowing grey beard, and unkempt hair—by her side was a dreary old man. Age had disguised the strapping youth she had first set her eyes on. Framed by the tree and its branches, gazing forlorn at the river as it flowed, they cut a dreary picture of old age. They were silent, neither had anything to say. Behind them the river flowed merrily, the cascade as it descended at its mouth roared with the same din. As though from nowhere, great white birds swooped midstream, unmindful of the current, their beaks poised for the picking. They reared and now jerked into the water with assured grace, emerging with fish in each upswing. As they rose, the sunlight caught a speck of black on the arching neckline. And then, just as swiftly as they'd come they were gone, rising above the water, fading into the skies.

The river bustled along without ever seeming to pause; here this moment, gone the next, carried forward in a blinding eddy. From the marshy riverbank to moss-covered stone to pebbles and rocks, it sped along in a flow of haste and forgetting. Vararuchi sat reflecting; there was no beginning, no end to the river. It was never the same from one moment to the other. As he sat watching he lost all sense of time. Woven as one was the past, the present, and the future in a seamless string of events. Yesterday, today, tomorrow—what were they but instances of a continuum that was itself timeless. The actions of today were coloured by the lessons of yesterday and brought to bear on the deeds of tomorrow.

The death of the twelfth child was a culmination in many ways. His principles were shaken; he was no more the arrogant, vainglorious scholar. Where earlier his actions were guided by reason and logic, now he was not so sure. His assurance had deserted him, the years to come looked bleak and forlorn. The fertile soil of their communion that bore twelve children had turned barren, there was never to be a springtime again in the lives of the couple. A profound, unmitigated disquiet dogged them wherever they went. The solace they sought was not to be found in the hermitage or the retreat. Nor was it buried in the wilderness or captive in the mountain ravages they traversed. The change of air or terrain held not a clue, what had altered was merely the circumstance. The seeds of misdeeds had rendered their hearts and minds cold, barren. In its frigid air, nothing thrived. They gathered their bearings feebly, the road of return beckoned; soon it would be sunset on the not-too-distant horizon.

But what of the one he had held hostage to his convictions?

Long, long ago a mother had cast away her newborn son at the mercy of the waves. He was found by a charioteer at the riverbank, who had raised the child as his own. Somewhere in that early estrangement was sown the seed of conflict. The child grew up to become Karna, the legendary warrior of the Kauravas. A reluctant hero, he remained to the end a tragic figure, a child marked by the hand of fate. In life as well as in death, he was a troubled memory, forever a cause of disquiet to his mother. The woman that sat before him was a mother too; how true had her choices been? At every turn Vararuchi had crushed her will with an iron hand. The hunched shoulders and withered countenance spoke of a terrible grief. The act of wrongdoing had cast a shadow on her. Indeed, misfortune had dogged the outcast girl since the hour of her birth. An elaborate deception had almost snuffed out her life at birth. The evil sign of the fifth day of the month of Ashweena, a perceived threat to the state, and the resulting ritual of sacrifice—all a pretence to further his ends. In his ears there echoed the chant of hymns by the riverside, and rising above them was the shrill cry of a wounded child. From that early episode until now it had been a tale of connivance, a not-so-subtle coercion that had all but crushed the little woman that sat by his side. Were she to have met her end in a watery grave at birth, perhaps it would have been the better for her. His heart grew heavy; a lump in his throat slurred his voice.

'Panchami!' he cried.

She started and turned to look at him.

'This river…do you remember this river?'

She was silent, her face wrinkled with nostalgia and longing. It was the river of her childhood, of a fonder time in her youth. Slowly she nodded.

He faltered, his words arrested by the look on her face. At length, he gathered himself. His voice was hushed, the words carefully chosen: 'The river of many beginnings. On its waters was tossed the accursed girl child to her doom, by its banks this sinner first chanced upon her as a youth. The rejection at birth, the first stirrings of love—it has seen it all. Amid tumult, amid change, the Shipra runs through our lives now as it always did. And quietly it flows, from then until now, mapping our lives to its course.'

Panchami sat listening with a mixture of expectation and apprehension. The despair and longing in her husband's words worried her. She rose and sat by his side. She laid his head tenderly on his lap and looked searchingly into his eyes.

'What is the matter? Why do you speak so sadly? Are you tired?'

The words poured out as Vararuchi wept. 'A farce, a sham! All my learning is but an arrogant display of knowledge. Never did it have a heart, it was always cold and cultivated.'

He continued in a tearful lament: 'We have lost everything. Dearer than your life or mine—the lives of our twelve children have I forsaken in this mistaken pursuit.'

Panchami hastened to console: 'It ill befits a man of your stature to indulge so in self-pity. Come, do not be so hard on yourself. Believe that our deeds shape our lives; what must be, will be. Take heart, perhaps the hand of fate has willed it so. Let us accept it as such.'

The words rang simple and true in his ears. He sat up and looked Panchami in the eye. It was a gaze of undisguised admiration.

'Panchami, great is your understanding, all my learning amounts to nothing beside it. Alas! That the moment of truth has taken so long in its coming. The years together would have been so much the richer for it. A world of discoveries, of experiences had awaited us.'

He gestured to the shrine, now in ruins. 'I would have made a home here and lived the contented life of a family man. Our home would have resounded with the sweet sounds of children and grandchildren. But now...'

His voice held the despair of a life lost forever. 'It is too late...too late. All the learning I sought has come to nothing.'

She laid a hand on his cheeks, stemming the tears as they rolled. 'The truth has taken its time coming. The insight of today is belated; if anything, it comes when it is too late to be of use.' Her fingers coursed lovingly through his unkempt hair. 'Come, to judge our yesterday with the wisdom of today is futile. Why despair over what could have been; as mortals we are not blessed with foresight. Surely, my wise husband doesn't need me to tell him this, does he?'

Vararuchi listened intently. A flush of warmth stole over his gloomy countenance at her words. Despair had given way to an expression not unlike awe, his eyes were lit with recognition. Through the tears he allowed himself a smile. Her words spoke of a fortitude and maturity he had never had. 'Panchami!' he cried, 'But I have you, forever mine—my wife, my child, my everything. You are my comfort, my reassurance forever; what a blessing to have you by my side.'

The outpouring seemed to have lightened him some. His body slackened, with a sigh he sat back, as though relieved of a great burden. But the relief was momentary; his taut frame shook as though rocked by a current. Arms flailing, he clutched at her forearm. His fingers clawed on her skin, frantically tightening; and then all of a sudden they loosened and fell.

'What…what is it?' She panicked; anxiously she felt his forehead with her palm. Her worry turned to fear, was his body giving way?

'I am tired…it's been too…' he fumbled, words faltering. Then, sensing her fear he added weakly: 'Nothing…it's nothing really. Just a little tiredness, that's all. This release… after all these years… it's like a spell has been broken.'

Panchami looked at him sceptically; she was not to be taken in by these words. 'A release, really? It was a spell of your doing. Why deceive yourself, hasn't it all been of your choosing? This life of suffering, haven't you brought it on yourself?"

Her argument had found its mark, he had nothing to say. For a long time he lay looking at her, transfixed.

*When had they first met?*

*What time had it been?*

All was silent but for the humming of the river in his ears. The waters of the Shipra coursed through a mosaic of memories. The month of Karthika in its ninth day of ritual and fasting. The fragrance of rasala flowers in the air. A glimpse of petite feet patterned a sensuous red. Anklets of a pearly white, trinkets swaying merrily with each step. The recollection was vivid; had it really been such a long time? The whirl of events was dizzying. And now…and now they were back where they began. The trail had led inward to the point that marked the beginning. The season of a flowering, the first stirring of love in a young heart. The long testing years dissolved; he felt their youth returning.

'We'll never know what age is as long as there is youth on this earth!' he exclaimed. 'Do you remember the day we first met; that song as you sat by the rasala tree in the afternoon?'

Panchami's face reddened. Eyes closed, she leaned backwards, her face turned to the sky. With an effort she steadied herself, her arms resting firmly on the ground.

'The old prayer song?' She was surprised that he remembered it still.

'It was a veena with a single string that rested in your lap as you sang,' he continued dreamily, 'I can hear your anklets lending rhythm, the little bells twinkling.'

'Lost, everything is lost,' she reminisced regretfully. 'Nothing remains, one of so many things we've lost as I grew up.'

'The loss of innocence as we grow up is inevitable, isn't it? But the beauty of the soul shines through circumstance; it makes its music faint but sure. Can one ever contain it?' He was insistent. 'Sing me that song once again, Panchami. So what if there's no veena, no bells to accompany your song? It is the purity of your prayer that I shall hear.'

In the wave of a hand the bleak landscape faded. It was the season of becoming, the onset of bloom in the tender bud that quivered with life. The ensuing melody swept through the veil of twilight that hung heavy in the air. Birds from high chirped merrily in tandem, the passing wind carried a fragrance of tender mangoes. The orchestration was complete. He listened enraptured, transported to another time. The mood was evocative, the occasion overwhelmingly nostalgic. The song ended, and with it, all suggestion of youth and love. In its place was a deadly quiet, a lifeless vacuum. She turned to look at him, tears had welled in his eyes. She saw in them an indescribable grief. Was this the Vararuchi that sought to unlock the mysteries of the universe, the science at the heart of Her workings? The very person that shunned without a second thought royal recognition and a life of luxury at the altar of his quest? The Vararuchi that cast away his children lest they come in the way of his seeking? What had come of those lofty pursuits, where was the man of legend? Her hands caressed his forehead, but he was inconsolable.

'Panchami! As I have sown so shall I reap. The sins of the past are being visited upon me.' His voice trembled with remorse.

'The end is near. I am but a wretched traveller who, having lost his way, misled his companion too. Forgive me, forgive this wretch, forgive, forgive...' He shook his head in dejection and broke down.

It was the moment of surrender; the man that lay before her begging forgiveness was not the Vararuchi she knew nor could accept. In all their years together their worlds had never met. He, the man of analysis and grammar; she, the one for abstraction and beauty. He, the steadfast seeker of a truth beyond her comprehension; she, the meek companion bound to his command. In her eyes, he was a driven, uncompromising man with a singular focus. To what end, by what means, it was never hers to fathom; her only duty was to follow him. Not once had she doubted his earnestness, the man and his spirit had held her captive. What she was witnessing was a crumbling of the image; the heroic character had become frail, all too human. There he lay revealed in truth; all pretence of strength and austerity had fallen by the wayside. With a twinge she realized how hard it must be for him to come to terms with the change. She wanted to comfort him but the words wouldn't come; it would be futile to assuage him with mere words. But the desire to ease his mind was too great, so she spoke: 'Come, come, in this living it is our deeds that shape our lives. What sense then of pardon or reprieve? Who is to ask forgiveness, and of whom?' The words came simply, holding genuine concern.

'Death is inevitable; everything that comes into this life must surely have its end. Perhaps your intuition of its drawing near is true. I have but a...' Her voice quivered, she had never been one to ask for anything. 'From the day we met, our lives have been one. For better, for worse, my destiny is tied to yours. Through deeds good and bad I have been by your side; we have borne our sins in equal measure. In this late hour, do not leave without me. As we've stood hand in hand in life, so shall we in death. In that ordained moment of parting, let us be together, absolved of our sins... again as one.'

He rose and laid his hand on her head. 'So be it, so be it.'

The plea had drained her. Her gentle firmness seemed to desert her; she slumped, resting herself on his back. He clasped her drooping chin and raised it, looking searchingly at her.

'Do not trouble yourself so; the twilight hour is for serenity and reflection. Not for wishes that lurk thirsting for fulfilment. If not consummated now, the soul shall know no rest, no peace in the afterlife.'

'But my soul is doomed to wander listless to the end, I know that,' Panchami retorted pitifully.

He pondered for a moment. Could he lend succour at this belated hour? 'No, that shall not be,' he was insistent. 'What is it that makes you listless? Tell me, is there a wish you want to see fulfilled?'

Resignedly she replied, 'To what avail? You were never able to give me what I wanted most. And now, what…?'

'But you were never one to insist, were you?' His reproach was filled with regret. 'Ask what you will, it is yours to demand, unconditional, uncompromising. Pray redeem me my word, this debt I owe you…before it's too late.'

'If it were the Vararuchi of old, the Vararuchi I knew; I would not doubt it. But the man I see now…can he really make it happen for me?' She voiced her doubt with certainty.

'The Vararuchi you see today is the same as of old. His running has tired him out; the doors of truth have refused to yield to his knocking. But make no mistake, his prowess and ability are intact. Upon my word,' his hands went to his chest, 'I'll gather all my strength, leave no effort undone in making your wish come true. Ask, do not hesitate.'

'I have but one wish,' her voice trembled with hope and trepidation, 'show me, if only a glimpse…my children, my dear little ones who are my everything. Can you?'

Her voice brimmed over with hope; the plea was profuse, fervent. Vararuchi was silent, lost in meditation.

'Yes Panchami, indeed I will. You will see all eleven, born of you and me, their features drawn from yours and mine. But for one…who was born formless.'

His voice glistened with pride: 'Each is unto his own, well respected in his endeavour. Loving, compassionate people; our ten sons and a daughter.'

She could contain herself no longer. 'Where are they? Show me now!'

He calmed her. 'We have to first pay a visit to our youngest son. He is today a formless divine being worshipped by millions from far and wide. They call him the Mouthless Lord of the Hill; an idol of peace and bliss, he is possessed of supernatural powers. Come let us offer our prayers at his abode, it is then that we will earn a glimpse.'

Reconciled each to the other, the couple took the road that led to the southern kingdom.

# Lunacy is a Calling

A well-worn path led into the heart of the thicket. The passage was dim and dotted with overgrowth of every description. Imposing trunks, gnarled roots, and overhanging boughs jostle for space. The floor was a treacherous bed of leaves and fallen branches. A hillock sat diminutively in the setting, with an air of quiet command over the wilderness around. In its womb was a child whose life has passed into greatness. A block of stone stood vigil on the hillock. An ethereal light cloaked it. Thick, broken lines of light revealed a flight of steps set within the mound. Heavy bronze bells framed the short stairway, the light dancing on their darkened rim. Vararuchi and Panchami lit the lamp at the entrance to the shrine. The dense silence of the thicket was broken by a shrill clanging of bells as the couple offered flowers in worship. Panchami bent down and embraced the rough-hewn steps, her body convulsed with sobs.

'Son, just once…to see you once more, just but once…'

Almost as on cue, a deafening clap was heard. A rumble rose, shaking the forest. The wind that began as a shrill whistle turned into a blistering hurricane. Leaves flapped wildly in the wind even as trees shook and crashed to the ground. Birds and animals, creatures of the night, were startled from their slumber and scampered for cover. Overhead, swaying trees stood locked in tussle, uprooted from their moorings before crashing to the ground, sending splinters flying in the wind. Above the din rose the peal of bells, growing louder and louder. It had begun to pour, somewhere the floodgates of nature had given way, the river had broken free of its banks, waves lashed in fury. The ghastly white of lightning struck; a distant thunder rent the skies. And then, just as abruptly, everything came to a standstill. All mayhem ended, the thicket was enveloped in a vacuum, a bubble of immense quiet. It floated, tantalizingly fragile, as if a nip of the passing wind would break the spell. There arose from the quiet a light. It grew in silence until it was blinding. As it descended the steps the outlines sharpened, the amorphous edges fell away, and a human form stood revealed. A finely formed youth of delicate features stood by the steps before Panchami.

Vararuchi looked on, dumbfounded at the spectacle. Panchami sprang to her feet and hugged her child. The weight of years vanished as mother and son were locked in a tight embrace. Her heart poured out. 'Oh, is the privilege never to be mine? How are your brothers and sister faring, wherever they are? It is a pity you cannot speak. But I knew that you possess supernatural powers. Could you, at least from a distance, give this unfortunate mother a glimpse into their lives?'

The shining visage remained silent; an arm reached out and turned the mother's gaze heavenwards. The late afternoon sky presented a window to the aftermath of a downpour. Black clouds drifted on the horizon, the inky background was canvas to a dazzling spectacle. On the twinkling firmament there shone the arch of a grand rainbow. Its colours caught the eye of a million droplets that hung in the air; the sky was studded with the sparkle of a million multifaceted gems.

Even as mother and son stood watching, the celestial chandelier began to dim. One by one, the lights melted. The dazzle appeared to sway magically, and in the wave of a hand, the sky was brushed with the colours and patterns of a verdant landscape. Paddy fields stretched as far as the eye could see; the canvas sparkled with green of every hue. It was as though a window had opened to a new world; the countryside of Kerala came alive in all its vividness. In a far corner, by the edge of the green, stood a dwelling of mud and thatch. A thick cloud of smoke rose from the roof. The air reverberated with a gentle hum as a chant rose from the dwelling. Inside was seen the master of ceremonies, a Brahmin youth immersed in prayer and ritual. It was the eldest son: Mezhethol Agnihotri. The vision remained long enough for the mother to transfix it in her memory. It was a passing one; the magical canvas shook itself as scene followed scene in gentle succession. The image changed and so did the central figure. Each bade his time on the celestial stage, each was a pride to his chosen calling. There now was seen Rajakan, the washerman washing clothes by the riverbank. Uliyanur Perunthachan, master craftsman and carpenter, scholar in the science of building dwellings for gods and men. Vallon, the farmer who worked in the fields. Now it was Vaduthala Nair, the warrior who gave way to Uppukottan, the merchant of the Vaishya caste. Then came into view Karakkalamma, ready-witted and a graceful dancer, the lone daughter in the family. Physician and faith healer Akavoor Chathan. Paakanaar, who traded in woven baskets and mats. The folk musician Paananaar, singing a merry tune to the beat of his rustic drum. And then there was the profoundly wise madman, Naaranathubranthan. Sweating profusely, he inched onward, pushing a steep boulder up a steep incline. Having reached the summit, he paused and heaved. A nudge was all it took to send the boulder hurtling downhill. His raucous laughter echoed in the hills, seemingly mocking the futility of all becoming.

A picture of contentment, the mother stood watching as the panorama unfolded. Her heart swelled with pride. Each had found a way in the world and in his native land, each in accordance with his temperament and taste. She was consumed by a sense of peace she had never known; her lips murmured a fervent thanksgiving. 'What a saga it has been! Am I the very one that was set adrift on the Shipra as a child? From then to this moment it has been a long, hard way for this poor soul. What all have I seen, what all have I endured. In my forlornness I had even reproached God for his unfairness—to what end this wretched life of a woman?'

'But now,' a sigh escaped her lips, 'everything is forgotten. I have seen my children; the divine moment is of your doing… God…'

# The Legend of the Hills

The air was filled with thanksgiving; tears of joy and redemption were shed. All hurt was healed, the ecstasy of the moment made light of a lifetime of suffering. The slight form of the mother by the shrine belied her joy. The despairing figure of old had given way to a picture of brimming delight. She turned to the luminous form of her youngest son. Her eyes were expectant with the yearning of a lifelong wish.

'My dear ones, I have seen them all, rejoiced in their well-being. Could I now see them, eleven brothers and a sister—siblings separated at birth—united in my vision?'

As though in consent, the son made a move towards the steps. A shining arm reached for the eave that hung low over the sanctum sanctorum, the bells that lined the eave trembled. The hand touched the smallest of them. It reverberated thinly, a tiny sound dancing in the darkness. It struck a chord with the air around it; wave upon wave now reverberated with a newfound intensity. The pitch had quickened, the bells appeared to beat to a grander rhythm. The air was filled with a rising murmur as the chant of the bells grew. As Vararuchi stood disbelieving, the air around them shook with the symphony, rising to a crescendo that danced off to the far corners of the horizon. The atmosphere seemed charged as though for a visitation. Her ten sons and a daughter appeared before Panchami. Each was with bowed head and sought her blessings.

'Mother, I am Mezhethol Agnihotri, teacher of the Vedas. Please do accept my humble salutation, and the fruits of my endeavour that I place here by your feet.'

The second: 'My name is Rajakan, and my calling it is to erase stains—be they from clothes or the mind. I place at your feet this silk shawl, please accept this, a little token of my profession.'

Came the third: 'I am Perunthachan of Uliyannur. Wood, stone, and metal are fodder to my craft. My offerings to you are the tools of my trade—a chisel and measuring scale.'

The fourth: 'I am Vallon, who works in the fields. These grains are the fruits of my toil and my gift to you.'

The fifth: 'I am the warrior protector, Vaduthala Nair. I uphold the safety and security of our race. At your lotus feet, here is my sword and shield.'

The sixth: 'Mother! I am of the Vaishya caste, the trader Uppukottan. I have for you that which is the essence of all things, which is ingrained in Mother Earth: a bowl of salt.'

Seventh to come was the only daughter of the family: 'Kaarakkalamma, dancer and singer; your daughter, Mother! I have but my anklets and a single-stringed veena to place at your feet.'

Eighth was the physician and a man of miracles, Akavoor Chaathan. He had with him the material of his magic—mystical shells whose formation foretold things to come, the wooden seat of his meditation, and a stick.

Spoke the ninth child as he made an offering of mats and woven baskets: 'I am of the Pariah caste, Mother! Paakanaar, whose craft it is to weave mats and baskets. Accept these, the products of my craft that I place at your feet.'

The tenth was a free-spirited soul, Paananaar, a poet and singer consumed by wanderlust. His sole accompaniment was a country drum, which he gifted to his mother.

Ten children had come forward; ten capable, righteous citizens. Each had found a calling that meshed with his nature and skill; in their union she saw the promise of prosperity. But there was one that stood at a distance, as though uncertain of his place in the reunion. His appearance was forbidding: thick locks of hair fell to his shoulders, his chin was dotted with a shabby stubble.

From a distance he spoke: 'Forgive me Mother, for I am a madman. They call me Naaranathubranthan, the contrarian who sees the flaw in all things. It has been my lot to see the world in my own eccentric way, in all its irony and futility. I make no pretence to being sane, no never. I am a madman whose madness is not lost on himself.'

The words poured from him in a torrent, the outpouring of a mind humble yet open in its innocence. Panchami looked at him, intrigued. His gaze was strangely compelling; there was in his manner a steadfastness that stirred something in her. His dishevelled appearance and fiercely etched features reminded her of a man who had fascinated her in her youth. The Vararuchi of old came alive in her memory. At the time, he too had been no ordinary man. In a daze, Panchami beckoned him closer. He came forward, hesitating; now he was face to face with she who was his long-lost mother. He threw his head on her bosom, sobbing uncontrollably.

'What have I to give, Mother, this wretchedness is all I have. Alas, for this waywardness hampers all intent.' Pausing for a moment he continued: 'And my Father and Mother who gifted me this...this...would they allow me to part with it?'

He felt the touch of a cool hand on his forehead. It was Vararuchi. The man who had stood detached and unmoving all this while, now reached for his long-lost son and drew him in a tight embrace.

'Son, your wretchedness is mine, this wretch that has fathered you; it is none of your mother's doing.' His voice was thick with emotion, his body shook with remorse. 'Call it a father's fondness for his son, if you may...it is the submission of a defeated man, a sinner's attempt at love.'

The children turned as one to look at the man who had been in their midst without their noticing. They saw in him their long-lost father; one by one they stepped forward and paid him their respects. Panchami stood watching, her eyes brimming with tears.

It was the moment of truth. The unspeakable act had bidden its time for all these years, his whole being quivered with repentance.

'Years ago, the hand of destiny had foretold of a bizarre union. That a Brahmin youth flush with fame and scholarliness would seek the hand of a Pariah girl. The foolhardy youth sought to thwart the workings of fate. He was seized with determination to change the prophecy; in the guise of a do-gooder he sought his revenge. He called for a venomous thorn to be inserted into the poor girl's forehead, who was yet a newborn. He then set her adrift on the Shipra, convinced that he had closed the dreaded chapter.'

Panchami stood stunned, disbelieving. What was she hearing? Nothing in all their tortured years together had given her an inkling of such a nature. He had, in her eyes, always been a man of fierce motivation. A steadfast seeker who viewed wife and children as hindrances to his pursuits. The length of their companionship had, however, given her fortitude. She was reconciled to his world view, skewed though it may have seemed. But never had she imagined…the revelation paralysed her. Shock, revulsion, and anger played on her countenance as she struggled to fully comprehend the import of his words. Was this, she wondered, the same impulse that had driven him to cast away their children one by one? She shuddered.

Vararuchi continued, it was the unburdening of a lifetime. 'But fate had the last laugh, she wove your life into mine as our paths crossed in an accidental meeting. It was a match ordained by fate, I realized it too late. Embittered but undeterred I carried on, determined not to be cowed down by fate. Vengeful, I forsook the children borne of our union. One by one I cast them away even as I suppressed untold grief at each parting. It was a father's love that came into conflict with his sense of duty. My single-minded obsession to overcome fate resulted in a lifetime of austerity and sacrifice. So has it been with you, helpless witnesses to my designs.

'But now the wheel has come full circle; I never could change the course of destiny.' He gestured expansively, 'All my knowledge, all my enquiry is an utter waste. The hollow badge of a scholar is all I have ever earned, but I remain a pauper in life and the ways of the world.'

Vararuchi looked at Panchami with an awe that shone through the remorse. 'What I could never attain with all my knowledge you have won over by love. A love that has come back to you in manifold measure.' Reproachful, he acknowledged, 'Today our children have recognized their mother in you. While here I stand tenuously, a stranger in their midst, a figure lost from memory. Panchami! You have succeeded where I have failed. That is my consolation, my hope of peace. All I ask is forgiveness for all that has passed.'

Panchami was shaken, her customary composure had deserted her. To think that the man, his manner, his bearing towards her was directed at something else. The revelation was shattering, it struck at the walls of her tolerance. Her eyes blazed as she looked at him, the limits of her tolerance were breached, she felt her defences giving way.

'What am I to say? That the man the world sees as scholar without equal is capable of such pettiness! What deceit, what selfishness lurks behind the learned exterior!

To say nothing of me…a lifetime of deceit, and to expect that I should forgive you! Indeed, my hands too are bathed in blood for I have been party to this heinous crime. And even if I were to forgive, would motherhood ever forgive me? In the eyes of history we are both sinners, partners in crime. There is no respite, alas!'

She looked at her children. 'A world to be born under their footsteps, this here is the new generation. Able minds and bodies devoted to work. Not for them the cold laboratory of learning, nor the perverse pursuit of the mortal soul. They live peacefully with their brethren, each secure in his taste and temperament. Their actions bring only good and prosperity to the world around them. Ask if you will,' a detached hand gestured to the children who stood by her side, 'forgiveness of our children. In their innocence you might yet find reprieve…' her voice trailed into uncertainty and resignation. She had spoken her mind at last; it was the reproach of a woman wronged by his vanity. She stood quivering at her own words. Vararuchi had gone pale as he stood numb, listening.

'Mother!' It was a rasping voice that came from the collective by their side. Vararuchi turned nervously; it was Naaranathubranthan. He shook aside his unkempt locks and stepped forward, there was something decidedly intriguing to his manner and bearing.

'Mother! My heart goes out to you. In all those moments of separation your heart would have bled with a wish—"just this once, if only for once…" The ache of your longing I can feel in my heart, as anyone who has feeling can.'

He now turned to Vararuchi. 'Father! No less would have been your wish to see Mother insist for once, that she resist with firmness, that perhaps, just perhaps, her insistence would win… But not once did the wish escape you, at every moment of begetting the words would have struggled inside you, afraid of finding a voice; hoping instead that she would oblige, that she would say no.

'But do you see what would have happened? All twelve of your children in the self-same mould of learning and erudition. Seekers all twelve, merely playing their part in the scheme of things.'

The earnestness of his manner held no trace of mockery. 'Nothing would change ever, the pattern would repeat; the same by another name, another lost generation…'

He turned to face both of them; until now, the words had poured forth in earnest authority, but now a trace of doubt crept into his demeanour. 'Tell me, Mother!' he cried, 'Is this…are my words…do they seem right to you? Or is it the senseless banter of a madman?'

Vararuchi was in awe of his son's understanding. The words brought him solace, he regained his composure. 'Son, the madness is mine, in my skewed vision for having attempted to see everything in its distorted light. That you should view it with such detachment and maturity goes only to show an uncommon intelligence.'

But the son hastened to correct him: 'Not of your doing, Father, rather the skewedness of time. It confounds our vision, blurring the lines between truth and myth. It comes

To say nothing of me…a lifetime of deceit, and to expect that I should forgive you! Indeed, my hands too are bathed in blood for I have been party to this heinous crime. And even if I were to forgive, would motherhood ever forgive me? In the eyes of history we are both sinners, partners in crime. There is no respite, alas!'

She looked at her children. 'A world to be born under their footsteps, this here is the new generation. Able minds and bodies devoted to work. Not for them the cold laboratory of learning, nor the perverse pursuit of the mortal soul. They live peacefully with their brethren, each secure in his taste and temperament. Their actions bring only good and prosperity to the world around them. Ask if you will,' a detached hand gestured to the children who stood by her side, 'forgiveness of our children. In their innocence you might yet find reprieve…' her voice trailed into uncertainty and resignation. She had spoken her mind at last; it was the reproach of a woman wronged by his vanity. She stood quivering at her own words. Vararuchi had gone pale as he stood numb, listening.

'Mother!' It was a rasping voice that came from the collective by their side. Vararuchi turned nervously; it was Naaranathubranthan. He shook aside his unkempt locks and stepped forward, there was something decidedly intriguing to his manner and bearing.

'Mother! My heart goes out to you. In all those moments of separation your heart would have bled with a wish—"just this once, if only for once…" The ache of your longing I can feel in my heart, as anyone who has feeling can.'

He now turned to Vararuchi. 'Father! No less would have been your wish to see Mother insist for once, that she resist with firmness, that perhaps, just perhaps, her insistence would win... But not once did the wish escape you, at every moment of begetting the words would have struggled inside you, afraid of finding a voice; hoping instead that she would oblige, that she would say no.

'But do you see what would have happened? All twelve of your children in the self-same mould of learning and erudition. Seekers all twelve, merely playing their part in the scheme of things.'

The earnestness of his manner held no trace of mockery. 'Nothing would change ever, the pattern would repeat; the same by another name, another lost generation...'

He turned to face both of them; until now, the words had poured forth in earnest authority, but now a trace of doubt crept into his demeanour. 'Tell me, Mother!' he cried, 'Is this...are my words...do they seem right to you? Or is it the senseless banter of a madman?'

Vararuchi was in awe of his son's understanding. The words brought him solace, he regained his composure. 'Son, the madness is mine, in my skewed vision for having attempted to see everything in its distorted light. That you should view it with such detachment and maturity goes only to show an uncommon intelligence.'

But the son hastened to correct him: 'Not of your doing, Father, rather the skewedness of time. It confounds our vision, blurring the lines between truth and myth. It comes to us in various forms, never failing to bewilder us—a burdensome past, a forgotten yesterday, an ever-changing present. Torn between the weight of tradition on the one hand, the fleeting experience of yesterday on the other, and the flippant moods of today, we are but mere gullible mortals. It is not surprising that we are misled, uprooted away from our true selves. That's all there is to it.'

The argument was expansive yet precise. The son had succinctly summed up the predicament of the human condition. The mother held her children close. Vararuchi advanced and made as though to caress Panchami on the forehead. When of a sudden, as though reminded of something, the hand fell. A wound of long ago! But Panchami stood unflinching. With bowed head she awaited his caress.

'It is your touch that I await. For my father who blessed and set me forth, for my children in whose warm embrace I stand; the loving caress of my husband is all I need. The wound that has held the ache of a lifetime—the time has come at last, it will heal.'

As he lowered his hands in blessing, the great and strong Vararuchi was in tears. Clutching her children, Panchami cried listlessly. The tears that rolled down spoke of repentance and of a love severely tested. They mingled as one and spurred onward in a current that knew no relent. Now it was a faint trickle, now it gained and grew into a bubbly spring, now it wound its way into a stream, now it swelled to a river…

The imposing Sahyadri peaks loomed in the backdrop. Below, the water had finally broken free at its source and coursed merrily through the valley at the foothills. A vista of green meadows hugged the foot of the hills. The repentant man and his forgiving companion were together again, reconciled for ever after. His tears mingled with hers as they flowed without ebb—and in its wake were borne the waters of a thousand rivers.

# Epilogue

The first flush of dawn lit the high ranges of the Sahyadri mountains. A faint tint of rose begins to wash over the snow-capped peaks. A gathering light faded imperceptibly into the scenery, gliding over the peaks, coursing down the valley. Edged darkly in the pale ambience, a solitary tree stood poised starkly on the peak's horn, not a trace of green on its branches. Its outline was dotted with flowers of a deep red in full bloom. The pristine silence was ruffled by a slow flapping, a laboured beating of wings. A pair of birds settled on one of the branches. They are the messengers of old, but gone was the sprightliness of their youth. On tired wings they bore the weight of years past, and the ache of a destiny long foretold. With drooping shoulders and laden wings they huddled close, each finding warmth in the other. The air was still, the skies cleared as billowing clouds vaulted overhead. All around were flowers in full bloom.

The male nudged his mate as he spoke. 'Here is Vararuchi. Cradled in the lap of the mountain, lush with coconuts and greenery is the land of Kerala, in the image of Panchami. The mountain and the meadow are together for ever after. Look, do you see the valley below with its meandering river? The river was once a little stream, that once was a bubbly spring, that had begun as a trickle that gained and grew from the flowing tears of Vararuchi and Panchami.'

The gaze of the male went far into the distance. 'Do you see life at the banks of the river?'

The female followed his gaze. 'A valley of riches, abounding in life and activity. See there, smoke rising from the thatched rooftops—wise men of the Vedas in ritual acts of worship. Washermen, carpenters, the farmer who cultivates his land, warriors, merchants, women in the arts—dancers and singers, physicians, faith healers, weavers, poets, and singers…and there are sane men who feign madness. Listen, the valley is filled with the hum of their daily routine.'

The mate looked on, curious at the spectacle. The male ventured: 'Do you remember what I once said? Of a race to be begotten by a Pariah girl?"

'Yes,' the mate replied quietly, 'of twelve clans.'

'What you saw is it,' said the male, looking at the riverbank by the valley, 'twelve clans born of the Pariah girl.'

The birds rose. There was in their wings a new vigour; they had lived their prophecy; all had come together at the end. Perhaps as they took flight, the wind beating against their chests, they smiled to themselves. Their flight sounded in the air for a long while; until little by little the beating of wings faded. The two became mere specks on the distant horizon…until nothing remained.

Down below the valley has stirred; the clatter of men and women at work is well underway. The rhythm and tenor of their work fills the air, the wind carries a hum. Wave upon wave it rises; the valley is abuzz with life. The wind carries snatches of sounds, vignettes of their daily living. Is that the tinkle of a dancer's anklets? The river murmurs in the backdrop, stone grates on stone hurtling down the mountainside. The wretch of Naaranathu is at it again! A folk drum sets to rhythm the strains of a veena. In the distance is heard a plaintive ballad; the signal of a new dawn. Sings Paanan:

*He has burst into tears,*
*our mountain Almighty*
*How the blue yonder opens up,*
*spring-scents in its downpour*
*The rivulets, the furrows*
*are gurgling, so's my little hovel.*

It is true. The river is swollen. Somewhere high in the mountains it has rained. Yesterday's rain…where are its beginnings, who had shed those tears…?